Other books by Sherrie DeMorrow:

Knight and Daye
Cloud of Dreams
The Elder Rose
All The Land
The Little Bird
Beyond the Land
A Little Princess
Romancing the West
The Silver Millions
The Painted Chapel
A Hound's Desire

A HOUND'S DESIRE

BY

SHERRIE DEMORROW

Published 2020 by

Lightning Source (UK) Ltd
Chapter House,
Pitfield,
Kiln Farm,
Milton Keynes
MK11 3LW,
UK

Cover Art Design by Sam Wall

To LL for help and support

In acknowledgement of LG, CE

and

To the memories of
RW, RL, LB, EB, EM, BR, JW

and especially TO'C,
who inspired this story

PREFACE

Although this could not be mentioned before, please be advised that there are sections of this book, as in the previous books, that contain *actual* life experiences, emotions and memories. In the guise of fiction, it is the only way to inform the public of the results of an extreme lifestyle and treatment toward a helpless child (now fully grown and *still suffering daily, the aftershocks of such treatment*). It is to be further noted that this individual suffers from a spectrum disorder called Asperger's Syndrome, which is a form of Autism. The author hopes this will not affect the enjoyment of the following, as well as the previous stories already written.

Despite the disclaimer in the aforementioned paragraph, please note this is still a book of fiction. The reader must suspend all preconceptions of belief in past history, as this book is not meant as an accurate representation of historical events (except in the case described in previous paragraph).

The historical attitudes towards sensitive issues, and people's prejudices of the time, had to remain intact to provide a sense of realism in the story. No historical figures represented herein had been harmed during the writing of this work. Any personalities referred to herein are used in loving tribute to them.

Some place names given are **NOT** real, unless otherwise stated or recognised as real (or based on real places). Other characters (for the most part) are fictional and loosely based on people known of by the author.

CHAPTER I

In a primeval past, I lay scrounging for understanding and light. Birds and waste flew in all directions against the stunning, green backdrop of the beautiful groundbreaking district of Cobhayr. They showed in all colours that reached as far as the Backnah Valley. The birds flew overhead, and the waste was under foot, in the street, as these unclean dark-age times were unclean. I saw my forefathers as an endless scream of conscience, just waiting to be heard. I saw my foremothers giving birth to them all...

* * * * * *

I, Conna of Cobhayr, the only surviving son of Longsearch and Caitshee, was born into flesh and blood in the year 627. It was an era of common magic, mystics and folklore, to which my dear dad subscribed. However, during this odd season of time, a fair wind was blowing to preach something new, and I was itching to find out what it was.

The era also boasted landlords, warlords, and tribes with their own Kings, who fought one another for dominance on one's land.

In the meantime, I thought we had it all. A small stone fortress was our home, built to our dad's crazy pleasure of specification. My mother made home brews, stews and told me to take out the trash every week. It was a closely knitted environment for all of us, drawn together through familial tragedy. There were other siblings in our oddball mix of personality, but they all died from something or other, before I was born. From the back of my mind, I could somewhat remember someone younger than me, once running about, then suddenly was no more. I was young then too, so the memory left only a vague imprint upon my mind. I could not remember this properly (nor wanted to), as the weight of existence rested solely on me now.

My dad, Longsearch, had a prominent life. No one knew his real name, if he even had one, as it was overshadowed by the formal, titled nickname of Longsearch. He was a King of the Cobhayr district of southern Ireland, located near what was referred to as *Corcaigh* (now Cork), the Gaelic word for marshy bit. He was a real hound of a man; the sort to see the light through burning imperfection. His face shone proud, like a theatre; all made up with somewhere to go. These early, pre-Christian times brought out the beast in all of us, and Dad was no exception. With the finery and fripperies of life, he became a spiritual pain to the gods. As his name suggested, Dad continually searched for meaning, and in doing so, his brain was always on fire, while still gasping for air. He burned with the fire of a true believer (believer of what or who, I could not say, for he changed gods like garments of cloth every day).

On formal occasions, Dad's grandiosity grew into a flourishing garden on a spring day. He wore the most sumptuous of garments which some admired, some envied, and others simply thought he went over the top again (the top of what, I did not know). His tunic was made of the finest golden brown bear furs, housed in delicately woven woollen knit, which continued toward his bottom half. The inner clothing was made of the sharpest linen this side of the Hebrides. Shiny silver bands enclosed his elbow and knee areas, along with his midriff, sporting a motif that showed his status. He wore headgear made of the same brown fur, with silver trim at the sides. The brown outer cloak had a braided pattern effect.

On more simpler occasions, he made do with a light coloured linen tunic, leggings, surrounded with fur, and enclosed in a dark brown earthy woollen cloak. He let his face grow out a little privately, and used his dirk to shave it off when we had company or in public view.

His visions were discriminated toward a glory of some kind, a strange heady mix of divine and self.

Most of the time, Dad got the two blurred in such a manner that it proved difficult to tell the difference. He tried to tell me about his experiences on a few occasions, in an attempt to allow me to catch that same fire...

... but as a child to the man, I burned on a different pyre.

My own primeval path lay before me. I never subscribed to Dad's craziness and told him so in return. He took no offence, but during a typical ritual one day, his fire burned too brightly and he was severely injured from it. It was unknown to which god he lit his fire at that time; he followed gods like a violent river flow. The mania changed with the tide, as there were many to choose from and he stuck to them all. In the injury of passion, the god had had it with Dad and struck a curse upon him and immediate offspring...

... thus so explained the reason I had no brothers and sisters...

... but then again, *why the heck was I alive??*

I had wondered about this on many a reflective past. I tried and tried to succumb to my own spirituality to find out the truth of my *own* existence. I found it frustrating that I never got an answer in return. So, between the both of us, neither could get it right.

Dad was well-intentioned, though seen as a pompous and a sullen bore by any god.

'Ho-hum,' the god would say aloud to his peers, 'There's that weird one; he's at it again, and getting it all wrong. Silly bugger could get himself killed that way...'

... and so on, as Dad was alit with self-imposed madness.

Mother turned a blind eye to his embroiled passages. She, like me, felt the new wind blowing. However, she was shielded from this by her continual worry and interest in Dad's ever changing spiritual schemes.

I thought I knew better. I was of age, and I disliked playing with anything dangerous, especially if it aroused displeasure of the Unknown...

... and it was that Unknown, I wished to appease in my own way...

... considering that It spared me from the fate of my would-have-been siblings.

Our family was still cursed from his latest action, as the god/s gave up on him; yet, Dad never gave up on *them*. Mother saw I embodied that lick of sense about me, and she bore her hopes upon me, in case he got into trouble again. We never worried about it, and classed it as superstition to look upon with distain and mistrust. Only Heaven's good guardians would help, and I put my trust in a more sensible manner of deity worship. I hoped someday to pursue that fair wind that rung the soul anew.

When our ends will meet, they will not be revealed so quickly, nor quietly. I reckoned we would fight it out for the common good, and die as kings and warriors. I had not planned to enlist, ha-ha, and so far, the land around us was reasonably peaceful...

... but for a few warlords and other Kings in surrounding regions who wanted to take over anyway. They left us alone, because Dad made a pact with them.

As I grew up amongst Dad's enflamed ardours, I learned the more common things a young boy should learn.

Hunting (land and water), frolicking (in case the occasional girl turned up), learning (to read, write, and practise intelligence of some form), and swimming (a must, for there was water around us, and it was another form of our deity worship to the gods therein). With the steady stream of life and personal devotions uttered daily, it was a good living, ending with a sing-song at the local tavern. Dad naturally dominated this, mostly when drunk and, as to please the gods, made a vanity dresser of himself, complete with mirror and drawers!

Youth was fleeting for me, as I searched endlessly for meaning in my life. I attempted to worship as Dad did, but I found it bore no fruit for me. I figured that it was *his* journey, not mine, but his desire was ever present, as always. In those heady days, I felt the air and wind rustle right through me, as I took my daily walk outside our home.

CHAPTER II

Dad was acting stupid as usual, quoting poetry, verse and plainchants in mindful drivel. His cape flew about inside a silent wind that needn't have howled...

... as Dad did all the howling for the wind and the gods.

Then, I overheard the endless rampage of verse, which rivalled a rampage of cattle that was heading our way.

I take in a mortal breath to release my soul,
Casting shadow, casting doubt,
I take no note of impudence
Of the gods reaching out
Toward me.
The far-off message came from a star,
Its points unknown
As light fights against paternal strain.

I went along and thought to myself that it was gibberish and carried on my way, never-minding the walk...

... as long as the horizon, that herd of cattle I spotted earlier was getting closer and more sure of itself.

I ran to grab my dad, who resisted at first, so highly strung by his inactions.

'No son, no son,' he cried, 'This is for me, I prayed for a Sign.'

"Tis no sign, Dad,' I yelled in return, 'Move it or you're dead!'

I had to carry him to a nearby hovel that was built upon our land, and sheltered there for protection.

The rush of the speeding bulk of animal was nothing to sniff at, and the air winced around us. The problem was that it was *our* cattle that flew by in a hurry.

'That Fynne again,' Dad muttered under his breath, along with his continuing ritualistic drivel I so rudely interrupted.

It looked liked the gods threw a ball of reality to him, which he caught before being flattened by it. His opponent, King Fynne, lived in the neighbouring valley of Kullducath, among many women and men he called his kinfolk. Fynne was as warm as deception itself, but Dad was astute, at least, with regards to property and possession. His mind was quick and sharp, but flipped just as fast into his dreamer state. Fynne always waged war with Dad, and fought against us. He wanted to expand his dominion beyond the valley, but Dad would never surrender his castle to him. The pact Dad made with the other warlords did not concern Fynne.

So what if Fynne couldn't get the castle? He could get something more dearer, the livestock. The importance of having livestock could not be emphasised more clearly. The herds provided meat and dairy products, as well for other uses as trade goods, a dowry, clothing, farming labour, deity worship, and even as currency. These animals were *that* valuable. So cattle rustling was penalised rather heavily, but for Fynne, nothing was sacred. As one of Dad's rivals, he didn't care, and had several men follow the cattle on horse. Dad knew *they* were the perpetrators, Fynne's men.

Dad was not amused by all this, as he exited the protective womb of the hovel and stopped them dead on. 'What are ye doin' with my cattle??!'

With no resolution as to why, the men dealt Dad a few blows, and intense fighting soon broke out amongst them.

He tried to fend them off, but was taken aback too hastily and Dad suffered a gash on the cheek. I hurried to the scene, preparing my sword to join in.

'These are my cattle,' Dad brayed, deflecting the other sword blows, 'My mark's on 'em.'

'Yeah,' answered one of the opponents, 'And where is it located, up the backside? We ain't lookin' there.'

'Here's to your backside,' I screamed aloud, defending Dad.

With a thrust of my sword, I did the fellow in. The other men looked around in panic.

'We'll be waiting for ye,' another taunted, then ordered his companion, 'Let's get out of here.'

The survivors had sent themselves in the opposite direction. Dad grimaced in pain, as his right cheek still bled. He cussed the crazy spirit folk that his age couldn't get him to act quickly against the marauders. He made an attempt anyway, and took out a concealed dirk to aim for one of them. It flew into one of the fleeing men, who fell disgracefully from his horse.

We ran up to that now-suffering servant of Fynne to retrieve his dirk from the side that it pierced. Then, Dad pounded in his head pretty harshly to finish him off. The dirk was placed in his brown leather scabbard. He took the herd and led it to one of our grounds men nearby, who penned the cattle where they belonged.

'You're a one man mob,' I complimented him, shaking his hand. 'Ye know that?'

'Yes. You see son,' Dad agreed, 'It's all in the aim. You aim high, you win. You aim too high, you end up like him.'

He pointed to the dead man. I took the point and learned.

'The problem is, Dad, your aim is to the skies.'

He turned to me. 'That is why I do what I do, and how I do it. The gods are out there, waiting for us silly mortals to pluck from their intelligence, some mystical whim called hope. I live simply, and I give and take as I please. But I never cross the line. There are some things you do not do. I shall defend my family, my fortress, and my honour.'

I then joked, 'And your sanity?'

He snapped at my rampaged comment. 'Hush, boy! Now, I'm famished. We'll do the shopping, shall we?'

He put his arm around me, grinning with an inane face.

'Mother's right, you are nuts,' I concluded.

'Takes one to know one, son, and I am the toughest of them all,' he growled back, sound and all.

He broke out in laughter, then fell quiet when he soon saw a small deer drinking from a stream. He focused on it, and snuck up behind. The animal couldn't escape Dad's dirk, as the blade ran a benediction upon it.

'Help me with this carcass, boy,' he ordered me.

I nodded my head, and was in total awe of his resourcefulness. We walked back home, as the sun began to set itself upon the dark path of night. I could see our home, our fortress, lit up from within, awaiting today's fresh catch.

Dad entered the room boisterously, and Mother shrilled, when seeing the cut on his face, 'What happened to you? Have you been hurt?'

'It's nothing Caits. Get a brew up, I'm dying for a drink.'

Mother then saw the dead animal on the floor and picked it up. 'What's this? A fawn?' She threw it back to the floor. 'Well, don't expect seconds, lad. You'll be lucky if I can scrape enough meat off of this 'un.'

'Ah, cut y'moanin' and get dinner ready,' Dad murmured. 'Conna, go help your mother. I've had enough fellowship with you for awhile.'

'Yes, Dad.'

I got up from the chair and took the animal outside to prepare it for the pot. As I shaved the skin, chopped off the head and limbs, I could see what Mother was on about. Fine, so there wouldn't be any seconds. At least we were damn lucky to have firsts!

As we were eating dinner from the hunt, Dad commented, 'That Fynne's at it again. He must be stopped.'

'With what? He's just scraping by,' I reckoned.

'He's one of the most powerful men in the area. He'll stop at nothing to broaden his horizons.'

'Then we must stay his horizon to where it belongs,' I suggested.

Dad smiled at me. 'How? What would it take to end Fynne's marauding?'

'Nothing that you can't handle, dear,' Mother stated confidently.

'Oh, thanks for the vote, Caits,' Dad rolled his eyes in sarcasm, but knew his dearest was rooting for him, as he took a sip of broth. 'By the way, this is delicious.'

Dad later put in a plan to stop the livestock raids on his land. He let me in on it, as well as some other local allies from the Backnah Valley. We planned a dawn raid on Fynne's lands and his remote castle. Together, we struck back at *his* herds, and divided them up amongst ourselves. Then, Dad had one of his men kill Fynne, which wiped out all opposition in the area. The castle was then emptied of any human life, at least to Dad's knowledge. Distant members of the family lived elsewhere, possibly under the same name, but posed no threat to Dad, because they broke away from their warmongering relatives. So, one of Dad's allies claimed the old castle as a second home, to provide for their extended family and offspring.

CHAPTER III

Over in the neighbouring Backnah Valley, lived a band of brothers, with their respective families. Multiply them with the endless litters of offspring, and you can get a reasonably sized tribe out of them. The brother's names were Lloyd, Lance and Lorne, collectively they were known as the Backnah Brothers.

They were noblemen/warlords, unlike Dad, so they were not rivals. In fact, they paid him tribute, and they were his best friends, but trebly rougher than him. However, they housed a practicality that Dad did not share with them, especially when dealing with the gods. Their pragmatic attitudes made way for sensible reason. They had weakened to at least one of the many gods, sticking to this one rather faithfully. This was evidenced at every dawn, after the night of a new moon, when a loud chant was shouted around the Backnah Valley. It evoked mystique and a mystery that surrounded their very lifestyle...

... *Mulhahrae.*

They sang out the god's name rambunctiously, awakening all life... Mulhahrae, the god of speed and agility represented as a warrior prince. In reality though, he was just an old man with a spiffy black plated, red trimmed chariot. He was a kindly, but distant fellow, always there when you wanted to get to know him...

... *in your mind.*

He never liked to manifest himself in a mortal sense, though legend had it that he did exist somewhere in the Backnah Valley, down Lansfalt Lane.

The brothers prayed to Mulhahrae with far-off chanting, incense burning and a display of good luck charms to fare them well. The most favoured time to show-off was just before a hunt.

A horn would blow to call out to others, announcing intention. Likened to a foxhunt, it was more brutal due to dealing with much larger animals.

And one day, Dad and I got invited to the testosterone-filled madness.

It was springtime in Cobhayr; a time when lords and ladies, or Kings and Queens, lounged lazily in their outer quarters, while the lesser men and women tilled the soil until it grew something. The only work the nobles and Kings and their families indulged in was in their prowess to kill. The hunting skill was passed down from father and son, normally, unless there was a keen enough lass to equally take it on. They trained daily, using bows and arrows, along with much stamina and patience. The dead animal was taken to the kitchens to be hanged, at the ready for the next feast.

The air was fresh and clean for a good hunting's day with the three brothers of Backnah Valley. I accompanied them, along with Dad to chase down the wild game and have it for dinner that night...

... or perhaps the next morning.

Meals didn't matter to Dad, as he ate whatever was put in front of him. For as long as I could remember, Mother worked hours on making the best meals this side of Cobhayr. There would be guests, too, as word spread around the neighbouring valleys about her skills within the lower orders of duty, despite her status. She did have help, but liked to participate as well. Mother rather enjoyed doing home-based tasks, and it was fun to work with someone else. It was part of an ecumenical existence we cherished as a family, even though we were one of the only families doing this. Most of our kind of people would never think to consider working with others, much less working in general!

Meanwhile, I set my mind to hunting, and stood on Dad's watch. I prepared myself for a grisly mini-battle with nature. My tunic and leggings were covered in light armour, and a helmet crowned me atop. A bow and a quiver of arrows, along with a sword were my main weapons. And a small dirk laid along my waist belt as backup...

... then, the horses arrived and there was no turning away.

The brothers Lloyd, Lance and Lorne stormed through the outdoors in full force.

'For Mulhahrae,' they all shouted in a chanted sort of way.

Dad joined in, shouting about within his own nonsense, affixing his star upon their horse-fire.

He turned to me and called out, 'Boy, aren't you comin'?'

'Be right there, Dad,' I answered, mesmerised at his overflowing audacity in flight.

I took my horse out to follow him, when suddenly, I heard an even stranger chant.

'Oh Conna! Oh, Conna!'

I turned around to see a lone figure on a nearby hill. I could not make out who, or what, it was. I deterred from the paternal path to go follow this new calling...

... but Dad caught me and was now livid. 'Conna of Cobhayr, where do you think you're going? Get your ass back here right now. We need you. C'mon!'

I was torn between the wishes of a fanatic and the call of a potential friend, who knew my name. *How did this person know my name?* It was fetching, though, no matter who it might be.

I decided to follow the certainty of Dad and saw the brothers and he get caught up in a death-defying wrestling match with an enormous bear. There was an intense struggle for the kill, as the beast had a nastier attitude than a pocketful of spiny quills. Blood trickled down for all involved, and the match had not ended when I arrived.

One of the brothers cried, 'Conna, come quickly. He'll eat us alive. Shoot him down!'

I couldn't make out which brother it was, and I knew it wasn't Dad, because the voice was different. I took out an arrow and prepared to shoot it from my bow. Elongated, sharpened claws struck out from the bear's paws, about to attack. I pulled back the bow, and shot my weapon...

... and missed.

'Conna, Conna. We trained you for this,' screamed Dad, 'Get movin' and kill this thing!'

A scream was heard, as the bear let out even more blood among them. I pulled my bow again, and shot the bear on the side. The bear winced in a painful distraction, letting go of the human opponents to remove the arrow. *'Twas child's play*, I thought smiling, *I could get this fellow, and Dad will be proud of me.*

The brothers and Dad ran away from the bear to regroup themselves and grab their swords from their sheathes. They chased the now wounded bear, who was no less aggressive. With four swords pointing at him, though, the beast knew the game was up and he would be killed. The brothers surrounded the bear, as Dad delivered the striking blow.

'There,' Dad said in satisfaction, wiping his brow, still working on the bear. 'I've got a new suit to wear to the Hunter's Ball, later this season.'

Lloyd was surprised. 'You still wear that golden brown and silver suit?'

Dad snapped in defence, 'And why not? I know. I'll give that old piece to Conna. It'll fix him good. I can have this lovely black fur instead.'

My youthful eyes widened at the prospect of wearing Dad's suit. I went up to him. 'Really?'

Dad got up from his kill. 'Yeah, son. About time you looked sharp and studded. Time for a lady, no doubt, too. You're of age, you're on a hunt so, go get 'em!'

I was astonished at his attitude, to which I replied happily, 'Yes, sir.'

I followed my heart this time, back to that hill with the mysterious being atop, who apparently knew my name.

CHAPTER IV

As I ran to the hill, Dad called out, 'Don't be late home, y'hear!'

I waved back in return, wondering why he was so *mother-hen* about me. A dismissive outlook soon changed the pace, as I raced to find out about this so-called wonder who caught my ear.

It turned out it was a young woman, roughly in her twenties. She was dark haired, wrapped in a sylph, raven-like beauty, contrasting with the light coloured linen dress she wore. She wasn't stunning to view, but she touched a comfort to the eyes.

She spoke out to me. 'Conna of Cobhayr.'

'Yeah, I am Conna. Who are you?'

'A fair maid to warn you of your destiny.'

I questioned, 'My destiny? Nah, I've been out with Dad and his gentlemen friends.'

'Some gentlemen. They're not the half-witted nobles from the Backnah Valley, are they?'

'They are, and they are far from half-witted,' I said, upholding the brother's dignity.

'Please yourself. To each his own and whatever.' She walked halfway down toward me. 'My name's Lyola, from Grantlee.'

'Is that a village?'

'A distant estate, if you will,' she murmured.

'Ah,' I looked up at the sun. 'It'll be nearing lunchtime. I've been out since early morning with Dad.'

She spat in disgust. 'You live with your parents?'

'For now, until I get someone under my own wing. Dad says I've got to earn them.'

'So you're a right domestic handful,' she commented.

I was shocked by her abrupt behaviour towards me, but I liked her. There was something feisty in her that reminded me of Mother.

I asked her, 'Would you like to meet my folks?'

'Too soon, too soon,' she dismissed. 'We'd just met.'

'The more, the merrier at the table, so it goes along,' I trailed on.

'I noticed you'd been hunting,' Lyola observed, seeing minor welt marks on my hands which indicated the use of a bow and arrow.

'You had a good eye's view of it. I was helping Dad and his mates.'

'Your father keeps odd company.'

I got intrigued. 'Why's that?'

'I hear those Backnah brothers at it with their crazy one word chanting.'

I laughed. 'You should see Dad and his ritualistic pursuits. He can be very comical to the unaided eye. He once set himself alight during the worship of one among his favourite pantheon. I know that would not seem funny, and he nearly got killed doing it, but his devotion is rather amusing. He changes his interests in them frequently. He is not attached to anyone or anything.'

'Sounds like a rather unhinged individual to me,' she snorted.

Lyola then ran down the hill, shouting out, 'Look at me, I want to fly!'

I took flight myself, to catch up with her. 'Was it something I said?'

'No, we only just met. C'mon, chase me. Let me lead,' she cried, now breaking into a run.

* * * * * *

My time with Lyola flew by these past few months, and it was nearly time for supper. It had been just simple meetings we had for the time being. I figured she was a bit shy, so I had put off her meeting my folks, until she was more comfortable with me...

... and so it was, when I gaily asked her, 'Can ye join us?'

'Don't have any better plans,' she responded, 'So yes. Remember, we only just met.'

'Hasn't our duration together been something?'

'I think so, yet we barely know one another.'

Lyola ran to our castle, the fortress we considered our place. I followed her, and saw a large gathering from far and wide that came to enjoy my family's hospitality. We took it in turns. One week it would be one of the Backnah brothers and their family to host, going through all of them before it got to someone else over the hillside. These gatherings usually led to parties on a royal scale.

I went up to the stone staircase, and led the way. Lyola held me at my side from behind to keep her leverage as she climbed with me.

I turned to her, once we reached the top. 'You're not used to this, are you?'

'Nope, my home's all level.'

'Like an oasthouse, I reckon,' I laughed.

I couldn't resist a joke, and my view was if you'd get with me, a laugh is what really counted.

I took her by the hand and we reached the doorway. I let myself in with the stringed key I had around my neck. Inside, a draught stung me a bit, as it reflected the coolness from outside. It was cold and damp in the winter, cool during the summer, and stifling all year round. The imposing ambiance would put many visitors off, but I got used to it, and I preferred to call it home...

... for if I did not, I would pack my bags immediately.

Lyola and I went into the kitchen where Mother was. A nourishing smell filled the air. A kill from our most recent hunting party was being prepared for roasting.

Herbs were ground to rub into the meat, which an odd servant had indulged in. Another one picked home-grown vegetation from a plot in the garden. Sometimes Dad would retain outside help, when huge feasts were prepared for his fellow peers and company.

'It's wondrous in here,' exclaimed Lyola.

'Thank Mother for that,' I smiled, then introduced the lass to her. 'This is Lyola of Grantlee.'

Mother recognised the name. 'Oh, that small place over the hill? I see. Nice to see you've got a girlfriend, finally. Lonnie was right, you don't hang about. Better get yourselves ready. Your father will be in soon with guests.'

Lyola stared at me quizzically. 'Lonnie?'

'Dad's formal name is Longsearch. What he's searching for, nobody knows, but he still keeps trying.'

I excused myself to get washed and changed and left Lyola in the kitchen with Mother.

'Anything I can help you with?'

Mother thought it odd that a fellow nobleman would allow his daughter to partake in the mundane...

... but it was nice to lend a hand now and again...

... *no matter who you were.*

'Sure you can finish rubbing this herb mix into the meat here, then we'll put it on the spit,' Mother replied.

Mother started to converse with Lyola. 'What brought you past Grantlee? I've heard folks up that way are rather private.'

'Oh, not much. I went for a stroll to escape the box. I saw your son Conna, and thought much to greet him.'

'I see.'

'It was not personal. I'm not trying to tie him down or nothing. Just wanted to bid him a good tiding,' Lyola explained.

'I'll bet,' Mother giggled.

They carried on with their dinner preparations when I turned up from a good self-cleansing tidy-up.

Mother saw me, as I entered the room. 'My dear Conna, you look rather fine today.'

I tugged at a silken sleeve of a lushly patterned tunic. 'Thanks.'

'Oh, stop fussing, Conna, it's smart enough. Your friend awaits,' Mother chided.

I greeted Lyola with a hug. 'Did you enjoy your time with Mother?'

'I did and I helped out.'

'The food here is good. You won't regret it.'

Dad then trounced inside, along with his circle of friends, struggling through a narrow doorway...

... and then put his arm around me. 'Conna, I must congratulate you on your fanciful gain. For years, this family had tried to ally itself with the family at Grantlee. Good on ya, son.'

I blushed at the compliment, when Lyola cried, 'But we've only just met!'

'So you say, lass, so you say,' Dad soothed, but the tone was intentional. 'It's a start, to end in alliance. And ye'll do as I say!'

We were taken aback by the darker attitude Dad displayed now. It was correct practise amongst families to scheme their way into relationships that benefited them, whether the match was prudent or not. It was all prudent and they could not care less what anyone thought of it. Lyola and I looked at one another and figured, as there were no other impediments than ourselves upon us, we agreed to Dad's terms...

... provided he allow us to grow together on *our* own terms.

I went over to Dad, spat into my hand and extended that hand to his. 'Done.'

He was chuffed and did likewise so. 'Hey, it's a match. There's no one else and time's tickin' away. You two make an excellent concern.'

Lyola got confused. 'What concern?'

Everyone fell into peals of laughter, rivalling the bells from a recently set-up local church.

Dad bellowed loudly. 'What concern, she says!'

His friend Lance of the Backnahs added, 'That is funnier than a head on a roasting pike on a hillside!'

Lorne could not keep still. 'Too much, Lon, too much.'

Lloyd was the only one who stood still about it, and congratulated Dad with a handshake.

With the merriment over, the men took their drinks to another room and began their cavorting, scheming and probably planning our wedding, too.

Lyola was still with me and I had her sit down in the farthest room in the house. Unfortunately it was the coldest, but it was winter, and we all came to accept this. The elongated chair was a shock to the bottom, with the fabric's chill ripping through.

She acknowledged her fate. 'Guess we've no else better to do.'

'You are correct,' I said, 'We are the greatest pawns for our parents. What about your folks? Would they allow this?'

'We are of compatible rank to you. I think they will. They'd been trying me out since I was fourteen.'

'Matchmaking ain't what it should be, then,' I rambled. 'It was good that I saw you during that hunt.'

'Yes,' she nodded quietly...

... I sensed something about her, though...

... something different, something rough...

... ah well, best naught to tell.

I thought about this new match with the lady of Grantlee. I knew it was not their real name; no one knew it, as they were a very mysterious folk, only coming out when needed...

... and getting Lyola 'out there' was their greatest need.

They lived in a style similar to ours, though not as imposing; nothing can be as imposing as our Cobhayr home. I thought about her family and referred to them as the 'Grantlees', for ease and convenience. Similar to us in origin (so we're told), they gained their status by rescuing a drowning lord from another tribe outside the valley. They retained to themselves and rarely attended any social seasons, unless there was something 'in-it' for them, such as a matchmaking.

Lyola turned to me. 'I don't know if I should say this now, Conna, but I am very fond of you. These past few months together means much to me. Now, with the families in agreement, there's nothing to lose. I have had fun with you, seeing you on the hunt, and practising sword-fights. This could work out well.'

The sentiment was mutual, as I then stated, 'I've grown fond of you too. Despite my Dad's willingness to make this match, I believe this to be a goodly alliance, too. I can love you too, to satisfy my heat, and my Dad's heat.'

'Huh?'

'My Dad's wish upon me,' I clarified.

'Please yourself,' she uttered, 'It's harder to please others, though.'

'Don't I know it,' I kissed her on the cheek...

... I didn't want to seem too eager...

... but there was a funny thing about Lyola that I was itching to resolve...

... yet, I decided to leave it for now. She will tell me in good time.

CHAPTER V

Some months passed by, and Lyola and I got married. It was a simple ceremony, based upon our old-style Celtic traditions. A harpist played a harmonious gentle tune, while a druid priest called Devenel led prayers and blessings over us, as we took our vows. Dad wore a horseshoe around his neck for good luck. People from the Cobhayr District attended the great event, only to be followed by a greater feast. This was supplied by my family, back at our place.

The Backnah brothers joined Dad in drinking themselves silly with folk from afar, which was a rarity. The occasion called for it, and the moment was enjoyed by all present. I had wondered about Lyola's family. They were at the ceremony, but silently mysterious in their presence. They left afterward, probably to ensure their daughter was finally hitched to a different mast.

I asked her about that, and it confirmed my thoughts.

'They just wanted to see me off. Pay it no mind, they're like that,' she scoffed.

My suspicious nature had risen further, but I had to put it on hold until our lives were more settled. Maybe they were private people; perhaps they didn't want to be known. To me, this wouldn't make too much sense, as when you marry, the families respectively unite somewhat. A wedding was a serious matter, and her family's absence at the party would have been questioned...

... if any one was sober enough to do so.

I remained sober, and stayed with Lyola. She was beautiful in her off-white sleeved gown. Her hair flew short in all directions. I wore a fuzzy tunic, topped with jewelled finery, bottomed by leggings.

Dad dressed up in his favoured golden brown and silver suit. The fur from the recent bear-kill would not be ready for some time, so he made do with what he had. Anyway, he knew he was big and wanted something to show for it. Mother was more laid back about it, yet was happy that I was at last wed. She liked Lyola very much and was pleased to see she was now part of our family.

For the meantime, we lived in our castle home, as it would take time to look for our own digs. It was spacious there, at least, if not draughty. Yet, we felt the parental cramp upon our style, and yearned for our own space. As much as I loved my folks, I had to focus more on my newer loved one.

So, one day, I took a horse and rode out toward Cobb's Reach. The hilly terrain wove the path and the turnabouts were most crude. I didn't go far, when I saw a mound with a cave entrance. I went inside to explore it. It seemed that the site was used as a dwelling a very long, long time ago. I saw some scrawls on the walls, so the need to decorate came with a minimal effort. The carvings were most primitive, and had a 'Kilroy was here' approach to them. The space was good enough for a central fire in the middle, with corners to lay some hay-stuffed bedding down. I could get supplies from home, and figured we could make something of this.

I then told Lyola about it.

She raised an eyebrow. 'Just a cave?'

'I would not say so. It is cosy and warm inside. Maybe a bit damp, but we could fix that. It could be ours, and we won't have to live with my folks,' I explained.

She squirmed in thought, as her face had a slightly distorted look, as she was deciding on what to do. 'Alright,' she agreed. 'A cave it is. Might make a good hideaway.'

'Yes,' I mused, 'We can call it *Oh Konn Nahh*.'

She gave me another one of her 'faces'. 'Why?'

'That's what you will be screaming soon,' I chuckled.

'Cut the shit, Conna,' she laughed, embracing me.

* * * * * *

We later moved into that humble cave of *Oh Konn Nahh*, and I gave her all I got. I found the sensations drawing toward something, but it was different somehow. I could not put my finger on what it was with this ol' girl. Yet, I accepted her and our marriage remained as solid as a stone gate.

We were getting on pretty well, and being the son of Longsearch proved to be advantageous. But, I soon found out, we had our drawbacks, too. Lyola wasn't pregnant yet, despite all my efforts. I felt ashamed and flustered over it. The minor suspicion I had about her became widened...

... but I dared not leave her.

I gave her time and stayed patient as I could, hoping she would breed soon...

... yet, for how much longer??

I was starting to look a bit like a fool, when Dad approached me.

'People are starting to talk, son,' he nagged at me.

I wanted to shout *it wasn't my fault* but kept still my tongue about it...

... so instead, I said, 'Yes, Dad.'

'I know it's not you, son,' he sighed. 'It could be nature, or you're not devoting your time to the gods.'

I turned to him, nearly confrontational. 'The gods have nothing to do with this. The matter is between me and Lyola. I've had an odd feeling about her for some time. I was hoping it would pass.'

He retorted sharply. 'And now it'll come to pass that you ain't breeding yet!'

'DAD!'

'Alright, alright, son. I won't interfere. But... what's wrong with ye, lad?'

'I don't believe it's me, but I sense something. I know I am with it, in regard to these matters, so it must be her, shan't it?'

He continued to point his finger at me, then walked away. We huffed and puffed at one another in frustration. I couldn't see how the gods could 'punish' me like this. Was Lyola the right one, or was there someone else they had in mind for me, possibly from a lonely future?

I sighed gravely, and focused my effort on Lyola. I kept her warm, fed her belly, and looked after her as best I could...

... but she still didn't grow some.

I screamed in agony, and bitterly wept at the sadness of it all. I had my time. I tried my best, still nothing!

Mother came to me with an ancient potion for both of us to drink. I didn't think you could drink yourself pregnant...

... but this showed some hope.

What did Mother put in that potion?

I asked her about it, and she threatened to kill me if the ingredients were revealed. So, I accepted the result, and kept my mouth shut.

'Just take care of your woman, Conna,' Mother advised.

It would be some time before any result came to effect. Some weeks later, Lyola revealed to me her cycle skipped.

'Something's in me, I think,' she continued.

I put my hand on her tummy. I didn't feel a flutter.

'You're not a doctor,' she giggled.

'Well, I'll take your word for it, but it better be right. Dad's getting under my collar over this.'

'Conna, I know you are important to your father; being his only heir means having the best for you. You are the last link in your lineage. I completely understand. I will not get in the way of it.'

She was correct about my being last link of lineage, and it got me rather worried. If I did not show for anything, then dear Dad Longsearch would be the laughing stock of Cobhayr district. That was a stock that could not afford to be taken lightly. His status depended on my actions with Lyola. I knew what 'having the best' for me was, but Dad's idea on what was best was to be determined by an unspoilt, third or fourth party...

... and I hoped this party would come from *inside* Lyola.

CHAPTER VI

Within the upcoming summery season, Lyola began to show further, and it looked like it was a definite thing. I leapt for joyful gratitude, with an excitement I could not bear alone...

... so, I shared it with my folks.

'Good on ye, son. I knew you could do it,' Dad exclaimed.

'I'm so pleased for you both,' Mother said, as she kissed me.

I still wondered what was in that potion of hers!

There was much nest-feathering to do at *Oh Konn Nahh*. I gathered some extra cloths and linens from the house. Mother was busy making endless fabric for us at her handy loom.

I joined Dad, with the Backnah brothers for another round of revelry and prayer...

... followed by a hunt, which they all liked doing anyway.

A boar was netted this time, and later on, Dad and I went fishing near the shore.

Much of the time passed well, and Lyola was taking advice from the local hag, Kitta, who was a teller, a seer, and a doer. She also had a blind, bloodshot eye, so seeing for her came mostly from within. Many in the township thought of her as a witch, or a sorceress, but the vast majority still needed her insight and advice. At least her dotty nature was reliable...

... and it was said that she had delivered a baby or two in her time.

Announcements in the district went far and wide, as King Longsearch of Cobhayr was about to have a grandson. Never mind that I was to have an heir! If it were a girl, everyone accepted it, but held their breath toward the next one. Babies come as a luck of the draw, which would rival the gaming tables at the harbour side.

The mystery surrounding Lyola was more intense, as she began to chant little phrases to herself. I'd assumed the utterances were purely devotional, but who was I to say? I allowed for her time alone, as she had to be prepared for the big day.

Weeks passed, anticipation filled the air, as more and more people stood watch to see the event to the end...

... and as it were, it was marked on time, and a baby boy was delivered unto us.

We called him Longjohn, partly after my Dad; the other, with invention. The child was a pretty, chunky sight, and all our neighbours paid their respects at the castle, which was the main hub of family activity. Many town and village folk brought us many gifts consisting of food, blankets, clothing, good luck charms, and some toys the child might enjoy. Dad was most pleased and if he'd have any cigars to pass out, he would...

... but he didn't, so he passed out the booze instead and threw another party.

Everyone drank to Longjohn's good health. The child grew rapidly in the weeks ahead, as all children do. Lyola and I nurtured the babe in our little cave of *Oh Konn Nahh*, with prayers, song, good food, and lots of love. Lyola had an unusual singing voice that Longjohn was meticulously attuned to.

I was curious about this, so I asked her.

'Oh, it's no different to others of the same nature,' she replied in return.

I smiled, my suspicions standing to attention. 'And what nature is that?'

Cleverly, Lyola responded, 'It is that from mother to child. A father wouldn't understand.'

'I see,' I accepted the explanation and left it alone. It felt elusive to me, yet I paid no heed to it. I wanted to be with my son and enjoy the joyful pleasure of fatherhood.

Longjohn became thrice the size after a few months, and after a couple of years or so, his height reached my knees. I loved a good run around with him, and taught him hunting, fishing and appreciating the natural world, with all the things in it. We brought home good meats, and Lyola set up a little spit roast to cook by. Our little family was progressing nicely, and I felt on top of the world.

* * * * * *

Later that year though, a massive infectious plague hit our fair shores, with a devastation that rivalled warfare...

... not that war was fair, you see.

It started with a case off the boat, an individual from afar came to visit. No one knew who it was, so it went unnoticed. With medicinal knowledge no further than the old crone with a cauldron (and we had that local one called Kitta), no one suspected a thing...

... until someone else caught it in a busy street...

... and so on...

... and so forth.

Cobhayr and its surrounding areas became prone to the malady, with most people keeling over, dying. It wasn't a quick death, but it was not slow, either. Out of panicky fearfulness, others ran for cover, but they too, died, being driven crazy from isolation attacks.

Mother and Dad were no exception to this, and they used their massive fortress of a home to bolt themselves indoors, laying in wait, or hope, for the illness to pass. Thankfully, their cupboards were reasonably full, but it did not take long for them to call on others to aid them.

Meanwhile, in my little den of *Oh Konn Nahh*, I was out foraging in the raging greens. Lyola and Longjohn somehow got infected by a passing wind. Lyola's sylphlike frame was snatched cruelly, away into thin air. Longjohn had disappeared without a view of goodbye.

Upon discovery of such, I cried and cried inside the little cave I called home. My own spirit was bereft of any amusement, and soon, I succumbed to illness as well. Oddly enough, it was not the plague that ailed me. It was the retching, aching, heartfelt pain, once felt in the distance when I first met Lyola. The yearning for her was unbearable then, and her loss now was equally so.

I thought long and hard about the dear girl and wondered. A sylph-like entity, a gripping conscience, a child who disappears *without a trace*. I paused and feverishly scanned my brain for answers. I searched within to find all the knowledge of my mind's experience...

... and it came to only one conclusion...

... Lyola and Longjohn had to be *fairies*, reclaimed by their masters of the fairy kingdom of Seecleare.

Good Heavens, I married a fairy!

My hurt soon became shallow, yet very real in my mind. This definitely explained my suspicions about her and that I had the right to be suspicious in the first place...

... but I still loved her.

The emptiness of losing a family was torrential, worse than a rainstorm on your head. I grieved for miles, while the storm of the plague ravaged the valleys, taking everyone within. Even the fabled Backnah brothers, and their respective families were taken, which would prove a huge loss to the area, and especially Dad, as he regarded them as true friends of his.

I stayed within the walls of *Oh Konn Nahh*, until the public horror subsided. Eating wasn't much of a problem, with animals around. I just grabbed, killed, cooked, and ate. Lyola's roasting spit became a firm companion to me in these leaner times. I didn't care what happened to me, but for every morning I awoke, I realised I had another day to live.

Soon the days shifted to weeks, and most of the time, I'd lost track around me. The majority of the population had gone under, like me, or gone under on a more permanent basis. I spent most of my time with spells of vigilance, prayer and scarce meat, and soon I made it out alive.

The physical state of affairs worsened as time went by.

My face was viciously caked with a beard I could not cut off, my hair was a complete wreck, greying at the seams, and my body was in no condition to enter a contest with. I only went out, sparingly, just to survive, hunting, foraging and hoping...

... when soon enough, a knock came to the door.

I answered, with a grunt.

It was Devenel the druid, with Kitta, the Cobhayr hag.

The druid smiled at me. 'Conna, you're still with us, man. We need your help.'

'Help,' Kitta rang out.

'What do you want me for? Can't you see I've lost my wife and child,' I protested.

'I know,' Devenel sympathised. 'May we come in?'

'Let's meet out here,' I went outside and closed the makeshift door. 'It has been too much for me. Did you know they were fairies?'

'I had my ideas about her, but I didn't want to interfere with your happiness, in case you really loved her. It was not my place to tell you,' Devenel explained.

I breathed heavily.

Kitta then chimed in, 'You are the only known survivor of high standing in the area, being the son of King Longsearch. We need you to run things.'

I screeched back, 'Run things? Are you saying there's not enough people to run a marathon?'

'Not even to attend a jury, my son,' she uttered quietly.

Devenel then proposed, 'We are planning to repopulate by bringing those from outlying villages that were not affected.'

'The only survivor of King Longsearch of Cobhayr,' Kitta mumbled to herself in awe.

My blue eyes widened, suddenly catching on to what Kitta was saying. 'WHAT?'

Devenel put his arm around me. 'There was nothing we could do.'

'Dad, Mother,' I wept. 'I know I hadn't visited them for weeks... I couldn't. Now I've lost two families!'

'We offer you condolences,' Kitta stretched out her hand to me. 'You can stay with us, if you like. You weren't the only one... many lost all, just like yourself. Kings, nobles, workmen and poor folk alike.'

I sat still in silence, and looked around me. There was nothing to keep me in my little hovel of *Oh Konn Nahh*, but it was still mine, nevertheless...

... but never minding that, I decided to break with it and move on.

I packed a small bundle, most of which was tattered anyway, and hoped another dweller would take over; it had been a most splendid existence.

CHAPTER VII

I ditched my young life for one of intense, mortal responsibility, as I took up my duties as the Successor of Cobhayr. I spent the next twenty years in the hands of the common people and noble folk, assisting with the running of our fair location. I did ceremonial openings, laid foundation stones for cornered buildings, served in endless committee meetings, and passed out an occasional marriage license or two. The feeling of being alone preyed on my mind heavily, and I deeply missed Mother, Dad, Lyola and Longjohn. I tried to cry it out, but the hasty offerings of life prevented me from beginning the process.

Thankfully, I had the Druid and the Hag to guide me through, helping me with discipline and fortitude. I lived with Devenel and Kitta in their simplistic shelter, and I was lucky they found room for me to move in. They lived in Iyadoo, a village close to the Iyadoo River, but walked around to make their presence known, in case someone needed help from them...

... and there were plenty of people who did.

Their place was a little like my parent's Cobhayr home and my hovel of *Oh Konn Nahh*. Not well furnished, they used clutter to keep in a style unto themselves. As learned individuals, there were scrolls upon scrolls, and some of them were used as decoration. The important ones hung proudly on empty walls, containing a prayer, a thought-of-the-day, or a fantastic never-to-forget recipe. They lived in separate rooms, and were always on the go. It was their prime shelter after a busy day, doing good for the world around them. The folks they served gave them gifts, acknowledgement, and payments in return.

Devenel and Kitta were an excellent choice of friends, as well as being knowledgeable regarding the affairs of this world and the next.

As unnerved as I was about Dad's persistence in his guiding my path, I slowly realised I took upon one of my own, and take the short step in the new faith of Christianity that was spreading wildly around Ireland.

One evening, over a pot of stew, I discussed this with Devenel.

'It's your life, son. Your path is your own now, but I'd keep a steady foot in the old world, if I were you,' he advised.

Taken aback, I saw nothing wrong with what he said, but I figured it was a *yes, you can do as you wish, but...* sort of response.

The stew was good and hot, full of vegetation and boar meat. Kitta prepared and cooked the meal, and it was apparent that domestic offerings were among her laundry list of multiple talents she possessed.

'I can sew, scan a mile for a meal, assist for curatives and deliver a baby or two,' she cackled.

Much of my days consisted of being in the heart of Cobhayr serving the public good. I didn't mind all the fuss it contained, but it was worth it. I worked all the time, except for Sundays, where Mass was heard in another newly built local church. It was I, who laid the foundation stone there. I named the place *Longsearch*, and dedicated it to Dad. The name fitted, as one's spiritual journey was one damnably long search. Dad spent years of his adult life trying to find himself, only to be driven away by illness. It hurt me so bad, but then I was free to choose my own journey, though I retained some portions of my wilder nature.

One day, when I had settled in my incubated space, Devenel and Kitta invited me on a fishing trip on their day off.

'It'd be marvellous if you would join us,' he said.

I agreed to it, and went with them the next day. We made our way to Iyadoo River, to hire a boat for the day. The gentleman-hirer was an old friend of Devenel's, who was once helped by Devenel when a family member had taken ill. The outcome was obvious, as the fellow happily loaned us the boat.

'Come on, ol' boy,' Devenel called to me.

'I'm here, Dev,' I answered back.

Kitta brought a basket of food and ale, along with some string and bait for us to use. We three had a good cast off, as the gentleman-hirer waved goodbye and wished us a fair journey.

The sun was out, the breeze was cooling (which was normal when sailing), as the beige coloured sail billowed in the wind. I overheard some scattered chanting in the distance. The words were inaudible; the distance was too great to determine them.

I turned to Devenel, who cried, 'It wasn't me. I'm preparing the bait with Kitta.'

I smiled and thought deep and hard. I was nearing my fiftieth year in life and it had been a long time running in the meanwhile. The plague, the death of my families, and the discovery that my wife was not properly human, had taken their toll on me. From larking about hunting with Dad, to stern municipal duties with Devenel was a very long pass to undertake...

... and I deeply sensed it was not to be my last...

... for there was far more to come.

I continued in thought about my parents, wife and child. Lyola was more prominent, because of her special nature. I wondered how Longjohn was getting on, and if the fairy world had complimented him. I still grieved for both because I missed them. I was more upset at missing out Longjohn's growing up. *That* hurt me the most. At least Lyola and Longjohn were still alive somewhat, elsewhere, and for me, it was a satisfying compensation.

Devenel cast his line out, after Kitta hooked the bait. He gave me a line too, and I let its string stretch outward. The waters were calm and deep. A shoulder pass was coming up and the boat took a turn off to a newer path in the river. Our lines were intact, as they gently graced the water, hoping for some activity. I likened the boat ride to spirituality, where the person was in a boat, floating on his faith, to see where it would take him.

A vibration shook me out of my daydream, as Devenel's line wobbled. I threw my line aside and helped him out.

'It looks like it'll be a big one, Conna,' he cried out, 'Can ye handle it?'

I doubted my ability; hunting was my first love, but I thought to give it a go. *It cannot be any different, really.*

'I'll have a stab at it,' I offered, taking his line from him. 'Take mine.'

Devenel did, as I concentrated on the endless wobble of tug. It was up to me to catch the great fish of the deep. I tugged, and tugged, grappling it with all my might, as if there was a war between me and that fish.

Suddenly, in another distance, a vessel emerged, with passengers aboard. I could faintly see many people stood up, and others entangled in their duties. *What was this ship doing on the Iyadoo?* I dismissed the thought and concentrated on getting that lovely fish from below. *A good catch of the day can fill a tummy*, I said to myself in jest.

Looks aboard the ship flew past our faces. Soon, I looked up and spotted another, a someone or something on that passing ship. It had the shape of a young girl, underdeveloped, possibly undermined. I'd have enough young girls around me in the town that I didn't think much of this one on the ship...

... but this one was different.

Because of the off-guard stance the young girl caused me, the critter yanked me from my boat, and I fell into the water. The fish hurriedly swam away. When the shock of instant wetness passed, I came to my senses, and the chanting I heard earlier became more extremely clear.

'*Cinniúint, Conna, cinniúint!* Your Cindihan is here,' the voices screamed loudly.

The words used were of our ancient tongue, referring to 'fate'. *But why pick on me?* I knew I was important in my quaint Cobhayr district, though I could not understand what more in store this *cinniúint* would have for me...

... Cindi-who??

I was surrounded by water, and got saturated to the bone. This was the sort of thing that would get you sick, so I was not happy in my present condition...

... when someone helped me up, and it wasn't Devenel...

... it was Lyola.

'Surprised, Conna?'

I felt like I was still living in a dream. 'Lyola, I thought you'd parted from this world.'

'I had and entered my own. I only died in your human sense. Are you hurt?'

'Exhausted and wet, and I missed my fish,' I lamented.

'Don't worry, it'll get caught later. I didn't want you to miss your fish for the sake of Cindihan.'

'But, who is this Cindihan?'

'She's your destiny, Conna. I had died from plague to remove myself from humanity, so currently you're not with anyone right now. You'll have to wait for her to grow up. She's young yet, but she will be yours soon enough.'

'Scratch my collar and put me in soap,' I muttered in disbelief.

'You are kept busy with other people's turmoil to worry about someone else right now. Go with it, the time will come,' Lyola assured.

Devenel reached out his hand to me and got me back aboard the boat. 'You alright, Conna? You look as thought you've seen another world.'

I turned serious at him. 'I think I did. Voices. I heard voices calling me and telling me of fate, and mentioned a Cindi-something. I also think that fish had escaped me.'

Devenel cursed under his breath, but Kitta's line did not miss the fleeing fish.

'Got it,' she shrieked.

'That was what Lyola just said to me,' I cried.

Devenel was surprised. 'Lyola? The one who died in the plague?'

'Yes. The one you married me to. I saw her after I fell in the water, but I also saw someone else.'

Devenel asked, 'Who?'

'Cindihan, Conna's now-intended,' Lyola stated, revealing her presence to him.

Kitta was keeping the caught fish netted up and waved hello to the otherworldly entity.

'I'm always away with the fairies,' she admitted.

Devenel still had disbelief in this infiltration of the other world. 'Lyola?'

'It's me, Devenel,' she said. 'I came to help Conna and to give him a message about Cindihan. That ship you passed had her aboard.'

He asserted, 'But that was a child!'

'I know. Conna of Cobhayr's a fine ruler, but even rulers have to put down the sceptre once in a while for someone,' Lyola remarked.

Devenel pressed on. 'Can't he marry someone in Cobhayr itself?'

'No. There is no one special enough to mingle with his destiny. That person was on the passing ship.'

I stood aback. 'Well, don't look at me. Who knows what this could mean for us, for Cobhayr?'

'She looks a handful,' Kitta uttered.

I shrugged, 'Why would I want to go with someone who's a handful?'

'Maybe that she could provide for you, Conna,' Lyola replied. 'Don't judge a handful meaning to be the wrong person, one in need, or anything like that. A handful could bring bounty to one.'

Devenel rubbed his chin. 'Never thought of it like that before.'

'I'll be seeing you again, Conna.' Lyola soon flew away to her world, leaving me with a new mystery to my existence...

... it was to be a vague passing...

... one that does not hit the shoreline that easily either.

I noticed my tunic was still damp from my ordeal in the river...

... and a voice rose up, 'There will be more to come, Conna.'

I flinched wildly, and Devenel calmed me down.

'What is it?'

I put my hand to my forehead. 'I don't know. Oh, what are your crazy gods up to? This is nuts!'

'They're your crazy gods, too,' Kitta warned. 'Don't tick them off.'

Devenel took me aside. 'Do you understand what happened to you?'

'No I don't. All I have is a name, a destiny and a whole head of questions.'

'It looks like you'll be interacting with the fairy world of Seecleare to get to the bottom of this,' Devenel sighed.

I dreaded the end to come, and we returned to the dockside, where that gentleman-hirer took the boat in. We left the vessel and my clothes were still damp. I was ready to relieve myself, but another relief was yet to be.

CHAPTER VIII

When we returned from the fishing trip, I was reeling from the visions, or real-time sights I had seen. It looked as if there was a long explanation owed to me, or at least something to guide me into understanding what I had just experienced. It was good that the company I kept in Devenel and Kitta would help me greatly, and that I was in good hands here.

During the meal which Kitta had prepared from the fish we caught, Devenel began the discussion I was awaiting.

'Conna, I know this will be difficult for you to comprehend, as it was for me. As a druid, clarity comes more easily. After pressing thought, and some time in meditation, I can safely say you had just experienced your meeting with destiny. The awareness of this young girl and her family has been revealed to me. The girl in the vessel you saw was Lowry Cindihan. Her family is known to us in the area, but they do not share our interests. They keep to themselves, and keep Cindihan in check, as she's their charge. She's a little young for you now, but someday, I foresee she will be your queen.'

Blue eyes met with blue eyes, and I shrieked, 'I'm not even a king yet! How could this be?'

Devenel soothed my nerves. 'Be quiet, son. The people of Cobhayr have seen you as their formal leader, as Longsearch's successor. Now, you will take your next step and become a king, as you are the last heir of his family, and all who opposed them.'

'What about Cindihan?'

'Oh yes,' Devenel steered the conversation back to the mystery girl aboard the boat…

… and continued, 'Cindihan was the girl on the boat we'd passed while catching the fish. She had been adopted by maternal grandparents, Hellid and Thallid O'Myde, the other two we saw with her on that boat.'

There was a hopeful surge in me. 'So the lass is Irish then?'

'Well, no. We do not know the original name of the family. They came from a Germanic region, so they're foreign. We nicknamed them the O'Mydes because of their foul nature. Every time they walk around the township, people usually respond *Oh my!*, and get out of their way. The name stuck, and allowed for further assimilation into our sphere of things.

'Cindihan's mother had fallen ill and died years ago. It was said she had the shakes, and convulsed everywhere at any time, with no fore notice given. The mother was a sad case; nice girl, too, so I'm told. She got with someone of Roman affiliation, who went by the name of Silardicus, descended from one of the Old Empire; a general, I believe by that same name. There is a faint possibility of a Celtic link, but we cannot determine where that bit comes from. The Celts originally came from the Germanic regions of Europe, and transformed themselves when they reached Ireland and Britain. So, who knows?

'It is most obvious the grandparents didn't go with the crowd, nor were they of those who migrated to these shores, but it is evident that Cindihan takes much interest in *our* surroundings and *our* culture, rather than in her family's. Just because the grandparents are of a peculiar nature (and unlike ours), it doesn't mean Cindihan is of the same. The people here know that, though some wonder about it. Yet, no one has anything against a child being tugged around by hulking elders, especially this lot. Children grow up and duly change. I wouldn't be telling you all this, if I felt she was unsuitable for you.'

'It sounds like she's being raised by only one set of folk though,' I surmised.

Kitta let out a cough, and drunk a bit of ale. She remained silent during our chat. She looked as though she was scheming something in her mind, and suddenly removed herself from the table to go into the next room.

'Yes,' Devenel continued, 'The grandmother, Hellid, had Silardicus chased off, and he was never to be heard from again. There were notices in the town enquiring of his whereabouts, and with no one responding to them, the adoption went through and the grandparents had full control of Cindihan.'

I wondered, 'Is Cindihan her real name, or a nickname like O'Myde?'

'Cindihan is derived from Cinder or Cindered Hands, as the young child suffered a ritualistic spirit-fire the grandfather participated in, that left her damaged hands, mostly on the fingertips. The name was then changed to Cindihan, to prevent teasing or the like. The Lowry bit is due to her being put down by others. It could also be another version of the name Laurie, turned into Lowry. We don't know. All I know is that she is a special person who will be with you when she is old enough.'

I was more puzzled than ever. 'A spirit-fire? That reminds me of what happened to Dad, during his rituals with the gods.'

'We all have our rituals, Conna,' Devenel said, 'And Cindihan's experience was no different to your father's. Her family have their own rituals, most of which have gone out of hand. Their idolatry is rife and worsens by the minute, as there is always something else to partake in. At the moment, I sense the child is being suffocated by her grandparents in that manner, and she is resisting them. She'll have to be watched from a distance.'

My mind reeled in as much as it could take. Yet, I had much doubt. 'First I marry a fairy, now you're telling me there is this girl, not grown up, who I'll have to wait for, and with an odd history to boot?!'

Devenel saw the look on my face. 'It's not that bad, Conna. She may be undeveloped, but I can sense a real bud emerging.'

'It sounds like you know the future, or I could be dead tomorrow, and that Cindihan could marry someone else in the meantime!'

'Shut up, Conna,' Devenel slapped my face. 'I have foreseen this. I'm not just a pretty face, you know. I am a druid! Cindihan is *your* tomorrow, not death. Just think, about thirty to forty years time, you will have her and create a whole new world with her.'

Now *this* I could not believe, and shouted rather loudly, 'WHAT!?? Are you telling me that I have to wait several decades before I have her?'

'Why yes,' Devenel assured me, 'The people need you as their leader, remember. You will become King Muffyhuer of Cobhayr.'

Now this was formulating on the ridiculous. 'MUFFYHUER???'

'It is to be your investment title as King. It means you are a hairy, positive sort. I note that you are quite hairy in the chest area, and you are brimming with happiness. The latter part of your title comes (shortened) from the French, spelt differently by accident. The former, well you know, fuzzy, hairy, cuddly…'

Despite the explanation, I still wanted to throw some punches out. *Who had the gods hooked me up with??* I let out a scream at all the madness around me.

Devenel asked me, 'Why Conna, are you perturbed by all this? By the way, do you still have that outfit with the furry texture that your father wore for formal occasions?'

'I believe so,' I reckoned, 'It must be at the castle, but it had been years. It must be moth-eaten by now.'

'Nonsense,' Devenel dismissed. 'With a little ingenuity, we could revamp it for you. Kitta here could help with that.'

The old lady returned with something in her hand, smiled at me. 'I can help you with something else, too.'

More weird shit? I groaned. 'What could you do?'

'This Cindihan sounds like a real catch. There is potential, but there may be trials ahead called growing up. What I will do for you Conna, is to see that you remain fit, for when she returns to you. Your body will no longer progress in age. You'll be advanced in years, which is inevitable, but you will be as healthy and handsome as you are now. I concocted a potion to still your age, and you will be fifty forever.'

I was curious at the prospect of keeping my 'youth' in some format, though I really wasn't that *young* anymore.

The vial was prepared and Kitta came up to me. 'You want to look good for Cindihan, right? Drink this, and as you are now, you shall remain.'

She gave me the vial. I took a sniff at the opening, and made a face, asking, 'What's it made from?'

Kitta replied, 'Now, if I told you that, son, I'd have to kill you.'

Now where have I heard that one before?

She continued, 'It may taste weird, but you won't regret it. Your newborn girlfriend will recognise you in future time.'

I hesitated still, yet, pressure hung in the balance. All eyes were on me, and it was up to me to determine the future, it seemed. I silently chanted a quick prayer, before I downed the contents in one gulp. My head reeled from a slight agony, which subsided, as I fell to the floor.

'Wow,' I uttered, shaking my head. 'What a punch!'

'That's not all,' Kitta advised, 'There is a side effect. You may attract a few more than just Cindihan. So I'd be careful if I were you.'

'What did you give me,' I insisted, 'Eternal Cuteness?'

'More than that,' Devenel answered, 'You've got a strong body, to go with it. No more than the usual, but the unusual aspect is that as you age, your strength will not diminish. It is health and look-all wealth for you, young man.'

I scoffed, 'Ha, me young?'

'Don't knock it. You're no lad, either. You are better. You are King Muffyhuer to-be, and will be preparing to make yourself ready for the delight of your life.'

Well if I were to wait thirty to forty years for someone to 'grow-up', *this better had be worth it!*

* * * * * *

I returned to the castle where Dad kept his 'best suit'. I had a go at digging in various dusty chests that hadn't been opened since the time when that plague hit our district. The dust lined my throat and I ran out of the room and hacked up wildly. I remembered the potion I drank and wondered if it would help me pass this irritation...

... and after a few minutes, my throat had cleared up nicely.

I ran down into the kitchen to fetch a dishrag and went out to the well and summoned a bit of water from it. I dampened the cloth well and put it over my face. Then I ran back up to my parent's bedroom to have another attack at their dusty artefacts and find that suit.

After some time fishing for it, the garment revealed itself under a load of parchment Dad kept for his rites and odd accessories my mother used to wear occasionally. I lifted it out of the trunk and discarded the wet rag I covered my mouth and nose with.

With one mature-eyed look, I chucked it over to the other side, and hastily cried out, 'I'll not wear this old thing!'

Hung-over with grief at my reaction and seeing a slight against Dad, I thought about reclaiming the garment, but not with total love. *I still left it on the floor.* The garment survived the years, somewhat, but parts of it (namely the fur), was moth-eaten and threadbare. I'd wondered if Kitta had a potion to still-time for clothing?

'You don't have to,' a voice came out from the hallway.

'What the f---,' I cried out again, astonished, when Devenel entered the room.

'Don't be alarmed, boy,' he said, 'Did I frighten you?'

'Y-y-y-you did, Dev,' I stammered unnaturally.

'It must be very trying for you to be here.'

'Yes,' I sat on the remains of a bed, now dismantled by hungry insects that prowled the room at night (presumably). 'I--I--I don't know what to say.'

'Say nothing, Conna. The ghosts are quiet today, but there will be more than just ghosts to fool around with. Let me get this for you.'

He picked up Dad's suit, as I put the other items back into the trunk.

'Naff, isn't it,' I dismissed the suit.

'Well, not really,' Devenel spoke hopefully. 'If we take the metalwork off, Kitta could sew on some new bear furs and presto, you've got a brand new suit.'

'Not my style, though,' I muttered.

'Doesn't have to be. You represent your family in Cobhayr, not only as heir to his lineage but heir to this district. No one will argue the spectacular display you will make wearing this.'

'I'll look stupid. It suited Dad, not me.'

'After Kitta refashions it, it will suit you, too.'

I spent the next long while thinking about what Devenel had said and offered me, and how it will affect the district.

I could not imagine myself, years from now, being married to a young girl with a mixed heritage, having a yearning for our own and something different from what she knew. *I only just glanced at her from the water!* If Devenel was correct in his sensing she's got a bit of Celt in her, then the prospect may not be as bad after all.

CHAPTER IX

With all the news received, I stood fathomless at the gate to another world. Revisiting my home after all these years was trying enough, but I confess impatience when it came to this match Devenel foresaw in Cindihan and me. I was not to see her for many decades hence, and my head could not conceive the possibility of meeting her again at all! I could not get past the notion, and took matters into my own hands...

... so behind Devenel's back, I went into town and pitched a statement on the church notice board:

Widower, 50, looking for a counterpart to share a world with. Please contact Conna, Son of Longsearch, Cobhayr Castle.

There, that did it. I breathed a sigh of relief and I went alone to the local tavern, *The Hopping Monk*, for a quick, stiff drink.

I didn't care of the consequences. My life was my life. *Alright, I was a leader, but, so what?* I still had my rights of destiny, and I didn't want to go by someone else's rites. I suddenly felt a kinship with Cindihan, as Dev had told me she was longing for an exit, too...

... *I guess we all look for the exit sometime in our lives.*

The drink was passed and I waited for the responses to come in regarding my advert. I thought it was a most bold one to produce, but hey, I've got to live too, you know. I was not just the son of Longsearch, *I was a man! I had needs, I had yearnings, I had...*

'Excuse me, is this seat taken?'

I turned to see who broke the trail of thought. A woman came up to me, with a friend...

... and soon, more 'friends' turned up.

To my surprise, my prayers were answered and the notice worked. It was only a near hour, when the word spread quicker through the township like lightning. The knowledge of the availability of the last, lone survivor of Longsearch was throbbing in the breast of many a single girl or widow, ranging from simple to intelligent, beautiful to plain, appealing to young and old. And it seemed that everyone in Cobhayr wanted a piece of me.

I attempted to escape that surrounding throng, when Devenel appeared and took me aside...

... far aside, back to his humble hovel.

To his horror, I had attracted practically every female bud in the district and, worse, they were *not* whom he envisaged with me. They were as unfit, just as they were possible...

... *but that wasn't the point, as I was about to find out.*

'Conna,' he cried, 'You have deliberately broken my trust in you. What were you thinking, telling everyone you're available and willing. In a notice, even! I took the liberty to have the damn thing removed. And I will have you removed, as well. How dare you have women barge through the door like that!!'

'For a seer, you have much to learn,' I quipped.

Devenel got very hot under his collar about that. 'This will not do Conna. I told you who is to be your intended. You betrayed my confidence in you, with you needlessly arousing all the females in the district!?! How could you!'

I smirked, 'I just posted on the board that I was available. I refuse to wait decades for some purported woman, just a child nowadays, undeveloped, unsweetened, unfettered...'

Devenel broke my speech, '... and most likely unloved.'

I felt for Dev's concern, yet I cried, 'It's preposterous!'

'You will do as I saw for the good of the District, our County and our Land! You will cease your tomfoolery and wait your turn. You are a King in all but name. When Cindihan comes along, you will be installed. Until then, you will continue to administer to our township.'

I stood up to protest. 'No. I want a woman NOW! I've already been cheated of someone by the plague and that it turned out she was a fairy lass! I must have a real woman. Not a child, nor fairy; a woman!'

Devenel asked me, 'Is that your final word?'

I huffed back, 'It is!'

I stood most proudly, haughtily at best. Never had we had a quarrel in all the time I've spent with Devenel...

... but his wishes for me were just more than I could bear...

... and the lack of female company at this moment was one of them.

Devenel then cast a spell on me. 'Sir, you may face your trials now. You are hereby banished from this world and will be taken to Seecleare, by my command.'

I suddenly fell unconscious. I knew it wasn't death as such, and Devenel was looking after my best interests. It was just my interests were somewhere else...

... and at this point, so was I.

I soon woke up, and it looked like I had been transported to another place, another time...

... or another world, maybe Cindihan's?

I looked around. Nope, no little girls with damaged fingers or the like, so I stood up, brushed myself off and told myself it was just a formulated nightmare to take advantage of my gentle nature...

... but really, where was I and where the heck were Devenel and Kitta??

The answer soon became apparent, as a gentlemen, as old as myself, with bright ginger hair and a kindly face came over to me.

'I am Ralstyn, the Sun, Sea and Heir of Seecleare, the Fairy World. You must be Conna of Cobhayr. We've been expecting you.'

Fairy world? I shook my head to reason, as I got up to face the fellow.

I was stunned by the fairy presence. 'You must be the leader, then.'

'Don't I know it,' Ralstyn smiled. 'I have been watching you ever since you'd married my daughter, Lyola.'

I shouted henceforth (*and with much forth*), 'WHAT? That's impossible. I saw you at the wedding. You didn't look like this.'

'One must conform to certain specifications to your humanity,' he explained. 'I had to appear different. Even our home of Grantlee needed to match your sense of worldliness.'

'B-but, but...' I suddenly fainted when a familiar voice arose.

'Father,' it said.

It was Lyola!

'It's alright. It's just your once Cobhayrian fellow,' Ralstyn said.

I sprang up to greet her with a hug. 'It is so good to see you. You're not going to believe what happened to me.'

She merely sniggered, 'Believe what?'

A throng of fairies surrounded the familial host of Lyola and Ralstyn, and let off laughter never heard by a mortal's ears.

I felt helpless in my odd-ball situation. 'Why are you all laughing at me?'

'Conna, you don't know?' Ralstyn put his arm around me. 'When you went fishing with your druid and hag friend, erm, it was to you to whom we were calling out. Those voices you heard. I trust the matter was explained to you. Lyola attempted to do so, but distraction was rife in those parts. You were not even listening. You just looked dumbfounded and unbelieving.'

I spat out, 'I fell into the water at the time, and was soaking. Is this about Cindihan?'

Ralstyn turned and answered, 'Yes. You will be with us to prepare for the event.'

'I thought I was to continue administering to my district,' I vented back. 'That I would be the next King.'

'And you shall, once you find your chosen counterpart of Cindihan and receive her as your rightful Queen. Not some town-tart who only cares about your status and money,' he replied. 'I got word about the commotion you caused. Those girls you picked up aren't even worth the coinage they'd spent on you.'

'Where's Devenel and Kitta? I'd been living with them.'

Lyola came over to me. 'You've been cast out from their realm of the real world. *You are now in our world.* Your naughty behaviour caused undue stress upon them, when all they did was to guide you since your folks had died.'

'But I was already a man then,' I insisted.

'No you weren't,' Ralstyn intervened. 'No. You were not the envisaged speciality we wanted. No. You must change, but you will not get your lady sooner. Good people are worth waiting for and Cindihan will be a breeze for you, once you understand her.'

'On a hot summer day? Not a chance. I've heard about her, and she sounds like hard work at a mill, with the stone around your neck. Her family are known to the town as pestilence. Who knows what claptrap they've posted upon her mindset. She might be so involved with their nonsense, that she can never be salvaged.'

'No way, Conna, but I understand your conundrum,' Ralstyn continued, giving me a good slap on the cheek and pointing accusingly, 'Word has it that the girl is *resisting* the 'claptrap', so it is obvious she refuses to believe in 'their nonsense', as you'd put it. Do not judge her, EVER, or by the family from which she comes. People change. We certainly do. She will also, in time. You will learn the better meaning of 'O'Myde' when the time comes.'

'But she's of different, mixed, and all that,' I protested. 'Her blood...'

'... is red like yours,' Ralstyn finished the sentence firmly. 'Your prejudice does not suit you, nor will it go unpunished. Cindihan will be just right for you if cared for, you will re-enter your world and then you will receive her into your Kingship of Cobhayr. Meanwhile, you are stuck with us for the foreseeable future.'

'And us little folk can see plenty, *so watch it*,' Lyola warned me.

I gulped a load of saliva down my throat at this intention. I constantly didn't, or couldn't understand why I was picked to live within the confines of *Fairyland*. After some reflection, I guess Devenel was rightfully sore with me and correct in his mind to punish me like this...

... and I wondered what Dad would have to say.

I was introduced into my new home, and I got to be with Lyola and Longjohn again. Longjohn's changed since my last seeing him, so long ago now. He's become an endearing fairy lad of his own; one whom every fairy lass would love to get her hands on...

... but wasn't that what I was trying to do for *myself* when I posted that notice in the church?

CHAPTER X

Life in this newer world of Seecleare, away from Cobhayr was pretty good, but it wasn't what I expected on how to live. There was knowledgeable magic about, nothing like the normal-folk superstitious folklore everyone grew up with, not necessarily to embrace or believe in. The fairies loved to play tricks on one another, or even on Man himself, for that matter. Their infiltration into the real world was one of their most favourite past-times, but when certain legal occasions would arise, such as marriage, it could get real complicated. The recent plague saved me from public humiliation, with everybody believing my wife and son were dead. *No... no...*

... they were well and alive in *their* world.

Another fun past-time for them was chanting sacred verse or mocking messages out loud for diversion and to gain attention. If someone was dumb enough to be led by the verses, they'd follow, and a spell would be put upon them, unknowingly...

... but, wasn't that what happened to me?

Oh hey, never mind... I knew I wasn't taken in by fairy nonsense. I had fallen in love with Lyola in good faith and I strongly affirmed to myself that she wouldn't have harmed me. It was just the early deception I didn't appreciate. Yet, we had a beautiful relationship and a child who grew up to be what he deserves.

However, I could not help but think whether I was still considered married or not. If I was saving myself for another, then what about the one whom I had before?

I went up to Ralstyn to ask about it.

He replied, 'No. You were married through human means. Lyola died in the eyes of the wider community. She is dead unto them, thus freeing you from wedlock. You can still be friends with her, though. We are able to infiltrate into your world to become one with you, but you cannot do so in ours.

I continued to ask, 'And why not?'

'Because we've got powers humankind cannot understand, yourself included. Though we're beyond your comprehension, you are welcome here among us. That is why we tolerate you when you are asking so much about ourselves.'

'Thanks,' I sighed, scoffing at the unusual experience I was subjected to. 'So Cindihan's the one, then?'

Ralstyn turned to me. 'You must now prepare for Cindihan.'

I felt worried. 'How do you know she will find me again? Will she even bother with me?'

'She will forget you, as you were only a passing glimpse from a ship. Still, you won't and we won't let you. Something will draw her to you.'

'Why is she so important that you defend her so much and insist she be with me? Why can't I re-marry someone local?'

'There are things you will come to realise in time, that this is the right course of action. A special person she will be, a forever child within her that will never die. You will come to nurture that inner child when she returns to you.'

Things confused me more and I simply dismissed the evasiveness. Not that I was unhappy with my hosts, mind you, but this business about Cindihan was proving to much for me to bear.

I decided to get up and take a walk, away from the dulling conversation around me. Ralstyn watched in silence and summoned Lyola to watch over me, just in case.

I looked around the new world of light and saw to its embodiment. I would give my full cooperation, if I could understand it all. There must have been good reason to banish me here...

... looking like an oversized, overturned turnip cart in the middle of Cobhayr Square.

I tried to develop my senses in this natural world I found myself in. I was looking at the foliage, the trees, the multicoloured flowers that grew all around me; their petals that danced in the wind. Suddenly, I'd walked too close to an embankment and I fell into the flowing stream.

Lyola was quick to retrieve me from the drink and asked if I was alright.

Sodden to the core, I gave her a look. 'Duh, what do you think?'

Giggling, she pulled me up. Of course, her intention was kind, but I still found it difficult to tolerate the endless silliness that paved the path of the fairy way.

I held her close, when she decided to fetch me some dry clothes.

'Don't bother,' I called out. 'It's warm enough, I'll dry out instead.'

She stopped midway, then returned to me. 'Had you missed me?'

'Yes I did,' I answered her, 'Though I was kept busy, and Ralstyn declared me free of you.'

'You are, because you are not a fairy. You have someone else to wait for.'

I went to sit down on a rock, as Lyola sang a small verse:

Was that a glance of a girl in the distance
So fair, so mangled, so distant?
Keep thy toes in the sand, and thy head in the clouds;
Pray love me, and make it go 'round.
The curve of sweetness is edged upon ye
A dagger's breath exhaled on thee
Make haste, make haste,
Thy hour is with me.

The rocks slipped away beneath me, as my butt-edge made its touch.

'Oweh,' it cried, rolling away.

I gave a puzzled look.

Lyola explained. 'Ah, you'd sat on a Catstone. They're a most sensitive creature.'

Sensitive to what? 'Hey, rocks are meant to be sat on,' I argued.

'Yes, but you cannot judge a rock by its appearance,' she said.

'A rock is a rock. They either stay put, or roll away, like that one did. God, you guys are weird.'

'Wait 'til you try the Catscones.'

I shook my head and sneered, 'What are they, a party treat?'

'Don't be so sarcastic, Conna!'

I had to laugh at the mini-ordeal I just went through. Then again, I still had doubts.

'What do you want of me here, Lyola? Why have I been sent to you?'

'Your little stunt in the town has cost you the next few decades of your life. You are to wait for Cindihan.'

'But I will not pay the price of age.'

'That's right,' she smiled. 'You will look as fresh and handsome as you are now to attract her.'

I uttered loudly, 'What is up with that girl?'

With no further answer to this, I exhaled sharply, sighed and walked away.

The grass felt soft beneath my feet, when a rope was thrown at me by another fairy.

I picked it up and shouted, 'What do you want me to do, hang myself?'

'No sir, you climb it,' the fairy answered, then flew away.

Climb it? This is getting too frivolous to bear. The rope magically stood erect, rising up toward a thick tree branch a few feet high. I began to climb the thing, struggling with all my might at every inch of it. I never thought my physical prowess mattered in the arena of love...

... and a love I had not known yet, either!

Once I reached that branch, I looked afar to another point, where a rope bridge joined the opposing side. The fibrous material was wearing thin and I was unsure of the bottom rungs.

Frustrated, I called out, 'Awh, what now??'

'You cross it,' the fairy called back. 'You use your hands and dangle yourself as you progress through.

I looked further, and I saw a small body of water. The rope served well as a bridge, if not for being rather tatty...

... and there was no convincing me. 'What is the point of all this?'

'To get to the other side. Just shut up, stop fussing and go,' the fairy goaded me.

I shrugged my shoulders, thinking of my times with Dad, and all the manliness flowing within me. I gripped the rope and pulled myself toward the other side. Unfortunately, I was not as manly as I thought and missed one, which sent me to another side, downward...

... and I fell into that stream below.

'Damn and blast it all,' I cussed wildly, rising from the water, and throwing a few more expletives in the rambunctious mix of words.

Soon, laughter emerged from the woods around me. Lyola came over to calm me down, saying, 'It's nothing personal, we're just a playful bunch.'

I sneered back at her, 'Yeah, I bet y'are!'

'Don't take your tone out on me. You have to be prepared for Cindihan by way of dealing with us. If you let little things tense your nerves, then this will all be for nothing. You must go back and start again.'

I harrumphed and returned to the starting point. I climbed the ropes again, and as I continued, I felt a very annoying, nagging sensation raging upon my body. My own sensitivities screamed out...

... and I'd let go once again into the water's end.

I rose up quickly, drenched in my own vexation. The crowd of fairies laughed even more; my patience with them being sorely tested. I was about to snap, but Ralstyn stopped me.

I yelled, 'What is going on? Why are you preventing me from going to the other side?'

'Endurance, my boy, endurance,' Ralstyn said, putting a finger to my lips, 'Not another word. If you are to win the young lass, you must show strength.'

'I am strong,' I argued back at him.

'Not strong enough. Desensitisation is the key. You also must be strong in mind, and not just in the body.'

I rolled my eyes in further exasperation.

'Now Conna, with an attitude like that, you'll never win the girl, nor understand what she's going through.'

'But I will not see her for many years!'

'No, you won't. But we can hone into her and see the suffering for ourselves.'

This now intrigued me. 'Suffering?'

'Yes, *the grandparents' abuse upon the poor lass.* I told you, she is repelled by them. You'll know when the time comes, Conna, now get thee back on the ropes,' Ralstyn commanded.

'You guys are playing tricks on me. You'll not throw me in the drink again,' I stated.

'This is not a tavern, but a testing ground,' he muttered loudly.

'Maybe this Cindihan doesn't exist.'

'Maybe she does, maybe she doesn't. You'd seen her and she has seen you.'

'Awh, she'll forget about me anyway,' I lamented.

'Perhaps, but she will save herself for someone. The Fates decreed it to be you. This is what we believe.'

I felt my anger and vented, 'Well, I don't! I'll not have you make a religion of it. I want out!'

'Conna, Conna,' Ralstyn tried to stop me. 'Would you rather be a boring administrative fuck-wit, like all the others, or do something really special for Cobhayr, and get ready for the most special person from the outside world.'

'Your world, my world, what difference does it make,' I sighed.

'Just go back to the ropes and do as you're told,' Ralstyn ordered.

I further harrumphed and returned to the ropes. After a successful attempt, someone gave me a plant to nibble on as a conciliatory refreshment. It tasted rather sweet, and juice-sap ran from it like a meat that's been drenched with too much gravy.

'It's a Catscone,' a fairy explained. 'It's got a hearty, smooth flavour, once you get into its stalk.'

I took more bites from the plant and the uneasiness wore off me. I felt more confident, and confirmed, 'You still won't take no for an answer, will you?'

'No Conna,' Ralstyn insisted. 'Your destiny is fixed and needs to be fulfilled. It is up to you how you do it. We are just showing you the way. You are the last of your human line, the one that counts in your world. Longjohn is one of us, and cannot inherit Cobhayr from you. Cindihan is your final hope and destination.'

'I guess', I conceded, still baffled by this all-important Cindihan.

I went back to the ropes and carried on my training for the day. I'd spent years in training, physical and mental. The fairies enjoyed the tricks of the mind, as well as titillation of the body. The material world did not matter here. I knew I lived a certain way, and adhered to different things, compared to what she'd been doing. Yet, in the back of my mind, these exercises I was given was the gateway to knowledge, that not many in my realm were exposed to.

This forced me to see things in a much different perspective. It was a perspective that would assist me in dealing with the one called Cindihan.

CHAPTER XI

Another aspect of my training involved the mind, and what was in it. The fairies felt it was important, as Cindihan was having a difficult time of it, I would have to prepare myself for emotional volatility. I still climbed trees like a primitive, making my way through what could only be described as an obstacle course. Fairy lads would chase me, fairy lasses would tease me; it was up to me to see where I was going.

The mental disciplines were a challenge and a half. A fairy lad called Malone was my teacher, who helped me acquire the acumen for getting into the heart of Cindihan's difficulties. I was told her social experiences were rather lacking in love and understanding; all she got was the burnt end of the stick. The fairies infiltration into the real world of Cobhayr revealed that her formation was stunting under the barrage of criticism she always received from those around her (namely the family, and those close to them). She tended to be distant from her fellows, and it wasn't good to be too distant. Very few people are called for the solo life, such as a hermit or a monk. Commonality should never displace Man. It's unheard of.

After Malone explained her situation from his in-crowd sources I asked, 'What shall I do?'

'Very well, Conna,' he replied, 'I pose this question to you. Imagine you see a frightened or possibly angry woman, taken to be young when in reality she is mid-centuried. You see her in earnest, but in stealth, as to not disrupt her fixed intention.'

I found the words odd. 'Fixed intention?'

He hit me gently, but firmly on the side of my head. 'Where the heck she was going, you dumb bombshell!'

'Do go on,' I whimpered, rubbing my head.

'Right. You see this flustered female approaching. She is in need of, say, directions, or a friendly chat. She comes up to you and...'

'... and I go up to her and ask if she needs any help.'

'Yes, my son, but you approach quietly. You tell her what she needs to know, if the need is directional.'

'But she is from Cobhayr originally, why would she need directions?'

'She'd left for some time, my sources say. Probably to get away from her folks. They left a terrible impression upon her which will be hard to iron out, if you take my meaning.'

I nodded. 'What would happen afterward? Would I let her go, or ask her for a drink?'

'That's up to you, sonny,' Malone laughed.

'Well, if I let her go on her way, what if she doesn't come back? If I am her intended, she can't have passed me up?'

'No, she cannot,' he affirmed, 'She will not. You see her on another occasion. You are sitting on one of the public benches by the Square. She walks up to you and decides to share space with you on your bench. Now, what do you think of that?'

'Why should she? Her, out of millions of women,' I moaned loudly.

'Your empty space is hungry to be occupied by such an illustrious creature,' he swooned, in an attempt to woo me to his ideal.

I resisted the notion, and cried out, 'Illustrious creature?! She's a bit of a head case!'

Malone became more frustrated with my attitude. 'Oh, stop being impersonal, Conna. All she needs is some tender loving care and a few hugs.'

'All fuzzy-brained, then?' I let out a chuckle.

He ignored my comment and gave me a grumpy look. 'She's got your attention now, what do you say to her?'

'Good morning,' I suggested.

'It's late afternoon, Conna.'

I closed my eyes and exhaled, 'Good day?'

'Good enough. What else do you say to this delicate little petal off the flower?'

I ventured another guess. 'In which garden do your flowers grow?'

He slapped himself, hand-in face disgust. *The girl's been traumatised by that garden!* Here, you can tell her how pretty she looks, or how long it has been since you both last saw one another. Maybe she'd been shopping and wishes to show you her treasures. Or you could just simply ask her out for a drink.'

'I'm not in the position to proposition to her,' I protested.

'You're not propositioning her, you are just seeing how she is, and that you would like to pass some time with her, with a meal or a drink. Maybe take in a poetic moment, listening to someone recite original verse, quite possibly her own.'

'Her own??? That's not possible; that is advanced knowledge,' I whined. 'I'm not even past the 'how ye do' stage.'

'Well, you better get past it, or you will look like a right mange in the Square. Conna, this is the girl you will build your world upon; your new Queen, when the time comes.'

I reflected on Cindihan's struggle. 'She's really that far gone?'

'Nothing that love couldn't cure; maybe a bit of fairy magic, too.'

I thought about it, then made up a scenario. 'Here goes,' I proposed, clearing my throat. 'Cindihan, you are fair as the sunlit sky. Have you been doing anything interesting? Would you like to join me for refreshment, for I do not care where you've been, or who'd bothered you in the past.'

'That's it,' Malone shouted in glee. 'You've cracked it. If you want to help her, let her come to you. She will in time, once the trivialities of introduction have passed. Make yourself available, so she's got the confidence to so do.'

I carried on my scenario. 'Whatever it is, it can wait. There's no rush for revelation now; when you tell me, you are welcome to burden this silly son of Longsearch with your troubles.'

Malone ruffled his thick brows. 'Now, you're saying a bit much there, but it may come in handy later. Remember to target her with love. I think I'd had enough for one day. I'll test you again later.'

I stared at Malone who walked by a small plant. He plucked a bulb and dipped it into water. The resulting juices were a delicacy among the fairy folk.

He asked me, 'Want one?'

I didn't refuse, and accepted his kind offer. We carried on discussing plans and ideas on the best way to handle the female in waiting. To handle Cindihan will be a tall order, but in time, I will grow to achieve it.

CHAPTER XII

While I was training for these many years, in body and in mind, little Cindihan came into her own...

... growing up the way she did.

How she survived such a crudely marked upbringing, anyone should surely guess. It was a most harsh, indecent and the most depreciating existence for her. The grandparents who took her in, had declared her father unfit, and her mother too sick to care for her. The hospitality took care of Cindihan's needs in body, *but what of her mind and soul?*

The ghastly Germanic gods the grandparents worshipped were most brutal in many aspects, one of which was the rites that were followed had led to the damage of Cindihan's hands. The damage did not hinder her, as it only stunted the growth of the tips; the fingers themselves remained intact.

The grandparents skilfully adopted Cindihan, and hogged her attention for years. They cared for nothing less than their own brood, which already had grown up and not else better. *Their children actually were worse!*

So dear Cindihan wandered about in her own mind, trying to find comfort and solace, away from the decrepit misfits presented by the closed-minded community around her. She had disagreed with the pagan austerity her family had demonstrated, and wanted to carve out her own idols to worship. She would even explore the new religion of Christianity that was spreading far and fast in Cobhayr and the surrounding areas in Ireland.

Her hunger for another path made her starved because she didn't get *anywhere* with the family. The desperation she felt with them grew impossible. Her feelings were never considered, and in reality, *who would consider anyone in this Dark Day and Age?*

She'd thought if there were those out there that might have given a damn about her, without the surrounding drama. Maybe there was someone; she hoped and dreamed of that someone...

... a someone closer to her that she could always dream of, who would later come forth into her life to care.

One day, she went on a short boating trip with her grandparents, when she was very young, probably about ten. She was dressed plainly, looked plain and there was no sparkle of the spectacular about her. Yet, there was something under the surface that kept bobbing up, and a quick glance of interest led her to the edge of the vessel.

She saw someone falling into the water from a small boat, probably one used for fishing. She can't have bothered to think that person would have shown consideration toward her. *No...*

... it was just a mere 'accident' that happened and nothing more. Someone wasn't careful; someone wasn't looking...

... and someone missed the fish.

She kept looking, and found someone else had helped the water-fallen. It looked like it was a fairy of some kind, but dismissed it, because it was too ludicrous to believe. So she took a final glimpse of the sodden fellow; turning away, she'd moved on, with the possibility to forget the incident and allow the passage of many year's time to take over. This man she saw was so much older than Cindihan, too, and probably had someone in his life anyway. The inner frustration of not knowing was compounded by the grandmother Hellid's insistence that she join them below deck for a bland, one-sided dinner.

The image lingered in Cindihan's mind for a time, but for the immediate spell of it, she decided to keep the incident to herself. In due course, the wet, older man she saw being rescued by a fairy was a minor footnote to be forgotten, allowing her to continue in the travesties of her upbringing.

Surrounded by elders and generational combatants, Cindihan stood alone in the forecourt of life. *Her peers were just as bad as the family who raised her, if not even worse.* The peers upheld the rules of the game, but whose game was it? The gods? The grandparents?

Those peers teased, and teased, then ignored, shutting her out of conversation when in groups. The cliques they loved to adhere to were most venomous and difficult to break into. The strength Cindihan shown inside was enough for her shortened fingers to make a fist, and even well-wishing to use it! She tried to give a 'look' of displeasure, but none paid attention. In fact, she had been further damaged by the family for being negative in the first place!

But then, who started all this, and where would she go, once all is said and done?

Word had it that Cindihan went away for a spell, but in a secret place. It was no wonder that this happened. The years with *that* family had taken their toll and she needed to break violently from their adherences. The decision was painful and sharp, but she had to act quickly. It was said that she went northward to the cold, or back to the Germanic homeland, wherever that was...

... and never mind about the Italian, for that didn't count for much, either. That lifeline was too distant, and she felt nervous about her father's family there. There also was a question as to whether they would accept her or not.

As she knew she'd never see him again, she dismissed any notion of hope in reconnecting with him, his family, *or even his culture.* Cindihan's father was gone for good (despite the blood link), and there would be a showdown of deeds, like un-minced words being put through the grinder, if he dared to turn up suddenly, to claim the girl as his own. No matter how many published petitions calling for him to claim her, it was too late to rescue Cindihan from the grinder of adoption. The Italian was duly thrown out of her life, carelessly and cruelly and the grandparents had the poor girl, good and proper until she came of age...

... but the torment would not stop there.

Over time, the people of Cobhayr were suspicious, but didn't believe in meddling in other people's affairs. They decided to leave well enough alone, but it was at the cost of Cindihan's life. Despite this, there were whispers about the town, claiming 'Thallid O'Myde had destroyed her body, but Hellid O'Myde destroyed her soul.' This confirmed *they knew* something was wrong.

Cindihan's life at that time was intolerable at best. She had to put up with *all the hot air* her familial elders had given her. Oh, if she were to be an elder too, she would change things greatly. Despite her wish to better herself, bitterness and resentment turned to pure hatred in her heart. She wished ill and no mercy on anyone and everyone, and the wickedness that the grandparents shown to her, had rubbed off on her. She soon stopped caring about others and felt very hard-done-by, *and very rightly so.*

Some Cobhayr residents were curious about her anyway, and wanted badly to help the poor lass. She made it clear to them that she could do it on her own, and had set out to do so. She did not want anyone's help, especially once she realised they *deliberately ignored her* in formative times, as far as she was concerned.

She shunned many away, and they regretted their not paying attention during the difficult years. It was no wonder the girl went away for the time she did, *as she felt rejected by the ENTIRE WORLD AROUND HER.* Yet, she didn't care about any one or any thing, and just lived to survive. She didn't care whether it was not proper to enquire of others, in order to help them. She was unconcerned with those who felt scared of Hellid too, as Cindihan herself was. Hellid O'Myde put the people of Cobhayr in a scary state of affairs that no one could untangle.

It was a huge burden to carry, but oddly enough, Cindihan wore it well. She felt if she had more control of herself, it would be alright. A few years away would settle things and allow her to have a good think about a different direction in life, as long as *that* family was no longer a concern. As long as society in general would **FORGET** the horrible existence she once had. She would love to have revenge against all those people who treated her so savagely. The native tribes of all Ireland were more civilised and humane, compared to *that* family which raised Cindihan. She really hated them, and all who were with them in deed. One day, she'll see to it that the ravages of time will go against her grandparents and all who stood by them, united in the cause to ruin the life of the young Cindihan.

CHAPTER XIII

There was a final part to my journey of training that I had to undergo, before I was received into the prime stable of Cindihan. I didn't know what it was, and the fairies didn't say much about it either. They now felt it was time for me to take leave and return to my place at the seat of Cobhayr to deal with the forthcoming situation. It was a real-world experience that they thought would be best for me, and informed Devenel of my coming.

Devenel now acted alone. Kitta passed on awhile ago; her features of magic would never be recreated again.

He and I had a long discussion about this.

'You know Cindihan's left Cobhayr due to her being driven away by the grandparents, who are now making a nuisance of themselves in our township.'

'I know,' I nodded sadly. 'I heard many of us are falling into the lap of the new religion of Patrick.'

'Aye,' Devenel responded, 'There are conversions at the local church, which you opened not too long ago.'

'I was thinking of pursuing this myself.'

The old druid's eyes turned ghostly, recalling our previous conversation on the topic. 'What? And give up the faith of your father's?'

I turned to Dev and confessed. 'I think it is the way forward. Don't you? You are about to make me the next King, you know. I must conform to my people's wishes.'

'Yes, but kings usually conform to their own drumbeat.'

I tried to steer the conversation back to Cindihan. 'So what about the grandparents?'

Devenel sighed, 'They are still clinging to their foreign Germanic ways, resisting the coming of the New. They are trying to make people remain with what was.'

'And it is obvious the common folk don't like it,' I guessed.

'It's worse than that. The whole of Cobhayr knows Hellid and Thallid O'Myde had driven the young girl away by their antiquated parental approaches.'

'Who wouldn't be?'

'Yet, they certainly know nothing of the spiritual, despite their black arts. Before the lass can return, we have to get rid of their dark blight and any other family belonging to their awkward clan. They are not one of us, though their name may suggest it. Remember, their name reflects our society's response to them of '*oh my!*'. Naturally, this does not apply to Cindihan; most of us had no problem with her. The fact she'd left us is tragic.'

'Yeah. Fine by me, but how?'

'Ah, that's where *our* magic could come into it,' Devenel smiled with a sweet glint in his blue eyes.

'Magic?'

'To use as bait for them. Before you assume your right to the Kingship of Cobhayr, you must show your people you are fit to rule over them, with love, fairness and swift justice.'

'Oh, the O'Mydes have caused *that* much bother?'

'Worse than that,' Devenel spoke with concern, 'They are trying to dissuade our township from their own spiritual voyages. There are many folk who are attracted to the new faith. No one should prevent them from having a look.'

I stared blankly at him. 'Are you worried your ways will be lost?'

'I know when the tide turns, Conna,' Devenel put his hand on my shoulder. 'It doesn't mean I have to force you to comply with it. You have your path before you.'

'And what is that path?'

Poor Devenel looked serious now, and it scared me.

'I want you to slay them, particularly Hellid,' he revealed.

So that's my task!

I shouted, 'You want me to kill?'

'Hey, hey, not so loudly,' Devenel tried to calm me down. 'It is a sign that you will not let your kingdom be ravaged by the beggary sort. A foreign sort is even worse.'

'But Cindihan is of their...'

'Never mind what she is, or what she was,' he snapped sharply and dug his eyes further into mine. 'It is what she WILL be that counts most, and she is destined to be your Queen. Anyway, I consider her one of us, akin to the same interests as the regular folk here. So, stop fussing about who she is, was, or where she comes/came from. Fuck the lot, Conna, SHE IS YOUR QUEEN!'

Damn, I never thought a druid would get so hot under his cloak about a woman.

I exhaled a quick breath.

'I'm sorry,' he said, 'I shouldn't have breathed down your neck about it. I know you are anxious about the whole business, but it is what you must do to keep your subjects at bay and rule as ordered.'

'Ordered by whom?'

'By those who came before you, duh,' Devenel replied. 'You are the son of Longsearch.'

This search of sanity would take longer than I expected.

'But to slay someone in cold daylight?'

'It's summer, Conna.'

'I can't go up to them, and say 'Excuse me', then unsheathe my sword and go *wallop*!'

'No, no you cannot,' the druid agreed, 'But this is where our magic could take effect. I will work on some of Kitta's old curse words and see if I could come up with something or other. Those grandparents are causing mayhem in Cobhayr, and the people are frightened and now complaining. *Society feels only you can break their sorcery.* This is your proving ground, Conna. I've helped you all these years, and everyone now wants action. They want you as their King, with Cindihan at your side.'

'So no one takes fault with Cindihan?'

Devenel rolled his eyes. 'I said earlier, no. They may misunderstand her at times, but if she gets over the initial influence, she'd turn out great. If it weren't for the hawk-like watchfulness of Hellid, I believe they would have intervened somewhat. Do remember, they were just as scared of her as Cindihan was.'

'Sounds good. So when do we concoct this plan of yours?'

'When the time is right, and your heart is willing to receive the sweet girl, you will know. My potion will sort them.'

'So to get Cindy back, I have to kill the grandparents.'

'Target them every which way, with no release.'

Now that I had something to work toward, I could feel a rush in my system and wait for the pleasure to arise.

CHAPTER XIV

Throughout the past week, I spent many an hour with Devenel, going over my training in the fairy world. The break from Cobhayr was needed, he felt, so that I could concentrate better, and the details of running Cobhayr were left to underlings Devenel knew and trusted. To help me out with the tricky kill, Devenel had found an old spell of Kitta's that used distraction and hypnosis, rendering the intended mark helpless under its power. He also thought a decoy would be handy, to provide further misfit against Hellid and Thallid O'Myde. Devenel picked Jannock, a life-long citizen of Cobhayr. After seeing many changes over the years, the arrival of *that* foreign family to the town proved too much for him, especially that *they* chose not to join-in with the rest of us.

Yet, Jannock was willing to have a good laugh at the expense of a bad apple in town, as well as seeing the back end of it as well. The decoy would be made up to look like me, though I had to physically strike the last blow against Hellid.

The small cottage where Hellid and Thallid O'Myde lived, was watched daily by a handful of the townsfolk. They were happy to play informant as to their whereabouts, in order to seek betterment of Cobhayr. The grandparent's activities were watched, and with the lack of Cindihan's presence with them, made it easier for them to yield toward their own destruction. When they'd appear in public, it would arouse the situation, and word spread wildly, coming back to me to play my part.

I stayed at my post in a small tower, overlooking the square. I discovered it not too long ago, just after I got back from my stint with the fairies. No one knew about it, though I would not put it past Devenel not to know about it. I usually retreated to this sanctuary where I did municipal business that did not involve the public. It kept me away, when called for.

I enjoyed my day-to-day task-mastering, and sometimes I looked over my shoulder to see if the old druid fellow would show up. One day, he did, and he sprinkled dusts of folly upon me, as I worked toward maintaining order. I knew he had a playful side, but his luck-follies needed to be entrenched to real luck, so I could circumvent the hazardous state in Cobhayr.

I read through scrolls of minor by-laws, enforcing most with my signature. It showed I was duly in charge, but not in the full capacity as a King. The people wanted to see me in action, a fighter, enacting laws that would lead the district against its current adversary.

I also looked for any justification as to what I was about to go through. Public disruption was one thing, but disruption on a fantastic scale was even worse. Perhaps this O'Myde experience was unprecedented. It was a unique problem for my age. It was made more challenging, because I had to gain the love of *an unwilling member of that family*. Cindihan had every right to run away to calm down, cool off, whatever; but the fact that she was to be a big part of a later life was something only fate, or faith could decide.

I shuffled through parchment after parchment with ruffled quills, when Devenel snuck up behind me.

'BOO!'

I turned swiftly around. 'Dev, you scared me. How did you know I was here. Better yet, how did you know about this place?'

My guesswork was correct about the druid knowing of this secret hideout of mine.

'It used to be a favourite of mine as well, I just didn't want to tell you,' he smugly revealed.

'Trust you. What do you want?'

'The family's out there.'

'I know. I am waiting for them.'

'No, silly,' Devenel spat, 'They are out in the square, now. The people are amassing and waiting for you to strike.'

I got up and tidied up my desk. 'Better than the man on the harbour. Guess I'd better get moving.'

'Jannock's waiting too.'

I asked, while fastening my clasp. 'Who?'

'You know, your decoy.'

'So let him slay them instead,' I scoffed.

'No, Conna, it has to be you.'

'So he's harassing them so I can go for the kill, right?'

'You got it,' he smiled.

I got up, strapped my sword-belt around my waistline, inserted the sword that hung decoratively on the wall, and strode away in a cloakèd manner.

I walked down the stairs, and into the grand outdoors, when I saw a gathering crowd stood before me.

'Conna, Conna, son of Longsearch,' they cried out to me.

What the heck did they want from me? I thought I'd given them good jurisdiction.

Then more voices cried further, 'Rid us of the black spells of witchery!'

Devenel came up to me from behind. 'Now's your chance; get yourself ready.'

Advice taken, I felt the usual lump in the throat, that then travelled into my stomach, as I passed through the crowded mess of Cobhayr.

Someone frantically greeted me with, 'My Lord!'

Others followed. 'Sire.'

'Our King,' another hopeful chanted.

'I'm not there yet,' I answered them back, appreciating the endless accolades I was given.

'You will be, son,' Devenel's shriek joined in. 'Now do your duty upon us!'

I raised my sword, lifting it gently and quietly out of its scabbard. Hellid O'Myde was shouting out her usual, soap-boxed, verbal tirade, as her other half scurried away like a coward-in-the-corner. *It became obvious that he didn't like her.*

The tirade was like white noise to the crowd, either through ignoring or heckling, which many of them did, especially Jannock, who hated their foreign influence on the town even more. More joined in, as Hellid found herself under a trance of some sort, that became further intensified, as I looked at Devenel. He recited from a bit of parchment, that had the distraction spell he was telling me about earlier.

I slowly went through the crowd, as people within yielded to me. A path was made, where I was clearly seen by all, and they knew what I was there for. From behind, I took my sword and cut down the gross, inspirited Hellid, in a manner befitting a hunt I once went on with Dad. Thallid stood silent and said nothing, accounting for the crimes of his wife and himself for screwing up the peace of the town, as well as the peace of their former charge, Cindihan.

Oddly enough, Hellid had no corpse. She poofed into thin air, as if she were a spirit herself. It was odd, because she was as clear and horrible as an unwelcome sunshine-day-in-your-eyes. I hadn't struck out that hard, and if it were up to someone else, they would fashion her demise just as efficiently. Yet, with Jannock's intervention and Devenel's enchantment, the killing became a spineless pointed meal to enjoy, even as she went *poof!*

The evil bitch was gone. The husband, Thallid O'Myde was declared banned from the district; even further so, the country. I ordered him back to his Germanic state of nothingness, where he remained 'til the end of his days. The family that followed them also was told to depart, but had been ambushed and killed when they reached the Continent.

The crowd cheered my action, as Devenel observed, 'Well, I didn't think it'd end that way!'

came up to him. 'No fuss, no mess. It was like they were transparent beings. A facade that had finally been revealed to all.'

And we did it, Conna,' Devenel shook my hand. 'Have Jannock recall Cindihan back to Cobhayr, where she will become your Queen.'

It was a momentous glory; yet I'd wondered how the fair lass was doing these days. It had been some time since I'd seen her, but time will tell how solitude panned out for her.

CHAPTER XV

Cindihan had nothing on her conscience, not even a fig, and no furtherment of memory. A passing wind inspired a renewed feeling in her and she decided to come back to Cobhayr, hoping enough years had passed and with further hope, that the family had been decommissioned permanently from Cobhayr. The message from Jannock reached her: *the people of Cobhayr wanted her back.* So, she turned away from self-imposed isolation, and returned on a ferry from the north, hoping she could begin anew.

Word began to spread of her coming and people were most excited. The townsfolk went up to her with happy intent, seeing the once, mispronounced person come alive, after all the years left behind. It was something to appreciate. Many were happy to report to her that the entire family's dead, including the grandparents, Thallid and Hellid, and that there were no further holds on her any longer...

... so the days of yelping and screaming had passed away.

* * * * * *

Devenel, oddly enough, was still around in his grand old age, yet nearly on his last legs. Kitta had been long dead by now, her position as mad hag of the town had been taken over by insignificance, and Devenel now worked alone. He sought out Cindihan, finding her in the old cottage where her grandparents used to live. It was kept neat, and clean for its time, by endless lodgers who came and went, saving it for her eventual occupation. Many soothsayers and spiritual folk, like Devenel, had convinced the local bodies that Cindihan would return and get with Longsearch's surviving heir, and to have a place 'fit for a queen'.

The municipality thought it was crazy to wait so long for Cindihan's arrival. It would be a shame to waste a good house, so they believed in the stories and silly folklore and rented the place out for years in the meantime. Everyone was excited about Cindihan, as she was foretold to return. Everyone knew she'd caught the short end of the stick and they bore no grudges against her, personally...

... but that didn't stop Cindihan bearing hers.

It was the work of that mangy, adoptive family that ruined her life up to this point. Since her departure, the townspeople had harassed and maligned Thallid and Hellid O'Myde, chanting the usual 'Thallid and Hellid and theirs, Oh My!' Many in Cobhayr thought well that she took a stand against that horrid Germanic family, even if she had to stand somewhere else.

It was a most happy time, and the news of the arrival trickled into the fairy world. For one last time before my installation as King, I had gone back to see my friends in Seecleare. Their teachings were most helpful to me, and I felt I needed to thank them by another visit.

I was eating a meal with Ralstyn, when Lyola came barging in, exclaiming, 'She's back, she's back!'

Ralstyn asked, 'Who's back?'

'Cindihan!'

I pushed aside my plate, knowing this was inevitable. All the time I spent training, and I still wasn't certain. *I did not know what to think.* I was extremely on edge over it, nervous as heck. I dreaded the time that I will have to face her.

Throughout my time in this fairy kingdom, I'd shown scepticism, with doubt riddling my bones as badly as malnourishment. I didn't want to throw a line over it, but I was wondering about the girl who would be a mainstay for the rest of my life. *I knew she deserved a chance.*

I excused myself, and left the table. I recalled the training I underwent, as I walked away in a reverie, and haphazardly bumped into Malone, the fairy who tested the mind's reflexive responses. It looked like he would give me a 'pop quiz'...

... and sure as security, he did.

It was difficult to forget such a character and his crazy methods, as he said to me, 'Now suppose you went up to her and she'd give you trouble. She'd not budge from the outset. What would you do?'

My immediate response was to kick in the door and leave, but he tut-tutted my action and told me to think.

'Come on, Conna, you know this one,' Malone urged me, 'She's had a bad day, a hard life. You're about to meet her. What would you say to her, Conna?'

I nearly pulled my hair out in agony, screaming, 'AUGH! What would you expect me to do?'

The fairy looked at me and told me, 'You must reserve your temper and take the girl in your arms. Never mind the befoul'd craft of the O'Mydes; give her understanding.'

'Just like that?'

He snapped his fingers, 'Yep, just like that.'

I muttered some more obscenities that didn't go unnoticed. A bucket of water appeared above my head, its contents spilled unto me.

'Hey,' I cried, now sodden to the skin.

'Serves you right for knocking the windpipe,' he warned, then took out a pipe to play a merry, but annoying tune.

'You won't get away with this,' I snarled.

'You'll not get away from your destiny, Conna,' Malone snarled back. 'Your father, Longsearch, tempted the gods, and look where that got him.'

'He was searching for his path. I am searching for mine,' I insisted. 'He died from plague. It's not my fault it all went wrong for him!'

'Or did he? Who do think gave it to him? Don't push us like children. You may think you are a speciality, which you are, but we can take you back to the scum ridden filth of humanity, and leave you there for good!'

With the lesson learned, I sucked up much pride and continued with further reflection.

The fairies decided then to return me to the 'real' world of Cobhayr and let me 'fight it out' with Cindihan. Though I would never set foot in Seecleare again, they cared for the outcome. However, the journey was now set to be mine and mine, alone.

* * * * * *

When Cindihan settled back into Cobhayr, people started to ask her if she needed any help. The evil from the town had finally dispersed, but nothing was done for her to ease the soreness of her mind...

... and it didn't help her having a smart mouth, either.

Her tone was sharp and it took folks aback, as if a storm hit. 'Why didn't you help me when they were alive, huh? It is too little, too late.'

'Don't brew your troubles on us,' they'd reply back. 'We just wanted to be sure you were alright and if you needed anything.'

'But why didn't you ask me then?'

'We dare not interfere, for fear of Hellid's magic. She had threatened us if we'd talked to you. She had too much of a hold.'

'What's wrong with talking to friendly strangers?'

'Nothing, it is just we thought she was doing what was best for you.'

'You thought? YOU THOUGHT??? 'Tweren't the best at all,' Cindihan shouted back, 'Now I'm messed up; and you are now, at last, caring for me? AUGH! It is too late! Nothing can be further done. I'm forever lost and damned.'

She stormed away from the small, concerned crowd, as I passed her in the street. Old Devenel was by my side.

'This is what you had been trained for,' he said. 'Your time with the fairies will soon prove its worth.'

Would it?

I shot back a look at him. 'You expect me to sort out this mess? Well, fine, I'll have a crack at it.'

'It's the girl and you must be delicate,' Devenel said.

'I know, I know,' I shrugged my shoulders, approaching the lass.

Cindihan was not exactly how I remembered seeing her. Before, she looked like she was controlled by someone else. Now, *she* was in control, and her outward appearance reflected so. Her hair was beautifully grown out and some locks pinned up, her dress was plain, but steadily bordered with intricate thread in Celtic design. I looked at her hands, and yep, they were still small, but agile. The familial injury had not taken hold on them in a bad way, at least they were useable.

I gave a small bow to her. 'How do you do, lass?'

She nodded her head in response. Something familiar filled her immediate senses, and a flash of memory came alive. She stared at me.

I introduced myself. 'I'm Conna, son of Longsearch of Cobhayr. And you are?'

'Cindihan, Lowry Cindihan.'

'Welcome Lowry.' I kissed the stunted hand.

'Call me Cindy, everybody else did.'

'Right,' I gave her a soothing smile. 'Been here long?'

'Got back from a long sabbatical up north. Felt like a wasteland. Didn't know the winters would be so harsh. It's good to be back, now the grandparents are gone. A messenger called Jannock informed me.'

'Yes, I know. You are forever free from the torment.'

She gave me a look. 'How did you know that?'

'I am the Heir of Cobhayr. I make it my business to know these things about my subjects.'

'Is that all I am to you, a subject?'

Our first meeting was not what I expected, and hadn't gotten off on the right foot. The left one was wanting, too.

'Hey Cindy,' I cried out, 'I shouldn't have put it like that. I'm sorry.'

She turned toward an unfamiliar concept. 'You are the very first person who apologised to me, and bring me sympathy. Everyone else just asked if I was alright. You did more, thank you.'

She left me and walked past the harbour, turning into a side street.

Devenel urged me on. 'Get with her, you dumb louse! She'll lose her footing with you and you will lose her forever. You must coax her to become yours.'

I made like a horse and galloped as fast as I could, with a sudden crowd chanting my name and cheering their lives away...

... now that was an unfamiliar concept for me!

I found that side street, but did not find her.

'Damn,' I muttered.

Devenel took me aside. 'She'll stick around. She's not going anywhere. There will be another time, Conna, but you must think fast to those fairy lessons. Swiftness is the key and to have her as your chosen Queen, you must prove worthy.

I wasn't sure if either of us were worthy for one another, but it will be worth it to try.

CHAPTER XVI

Taking the advice of many, I squeezed in some time with Cindihan, during my usual workday. I took her to my secret tower (which wasn't much of a secret, as Devenel knew about it, too), and we spent my less harried spells of the day confiding in one another...

... and there was much to confide about, though how it was expressed was an oddly different matter.

I remembered what Malone said about winning the girl over, sort of like on a date...

... but this was no date...

... it was to become serious love.

I gave the fairies my all-out endurance, while I learned to give Cindihan my tender endearance. I then sat her down in one of my large, round-backed, comfy chairs, so as to get her in the mood and start talking.

And being as brave as I thought I was, I began:

'For sound, I've watched thee
Come hither and unburden thyself to me
A curse upon the quietest passing ship,
A ship that carried a fair maid,
A young maid,
Too young to be wed.
I wish it were your flesh I kiss
and not my hand, nor pillow to be.'

I think Malone would have been proud with that.

To which Cindihan replied, 'So you're the man I saw in motion; I rave upon ye.'

I continued:
'A voice awakens I know not how
Like writing a bauble in the night
Come next morning, you cannot read it.'

She then went on:
'I see thee in a room where lovers breed,
A stirring, grey haired map of a man.
Upon this mortal soil this bandwith reach,
I renewed my vow, as I was well-endowed.'

I then asked, 'Why did I wait for you, for so long?'

She answered, 'Growing up is hard to do.'

'We're an island of many doings and many districts; many kings rule them all. I am about to become one of them, if you be my Queen. I confess to ye that I've slain the old cow, so you can get a life and have me. It was foretold.'

'Oh, so that's what happened to that horrible witch. When the man of your dreams awakens by the sound of a fairy's bell, I knew it was time to come back,' she sighed, now enlightened.

'If that is so, then I can lift my face to the clouds, and be proud of who I am.'

'Well, if you're to be a king, then the sentiment rings true. I would be proud to be your subject.'

'And my Queen, my love,' I lent over and gave her a kiss.

'I spat at false faith,' she cried, 'My love for you cannot wait!'

We kissed more closely...

Thou murderous production, by tulip's passion!
Thou rubs brains against thyself?
The bountiful mental effluence,
Sweet germs upon ye now!

I further cried out:
'I've hooted and hollered by the name,
The one bequeathed, not yet fifty
Aye, your time's frozen, frozen into your beauty.
Ye shall not age beyond your prime,
But shall be yet alive.'

She looked at me with hope:
'I lay stagnant 'til month's end
Since the last one came,
I pray to my greatest god to find my greatest love.
Days of discretion were getting to me
Thou tutored me out from quarantine,
As shouted lines from a play
Lay disbanded at my feet.'

I then quipped:
'You need a good den to rest in
Upon a corner toward Bouncy Square
You use your swords like guns;
'Tis a scene of blurred vision.

'All the thoughts flew to dust,
A play's fair meat for a troubled quarantine.'

'A fair meat,' she repeated further:
'I thought not it fair!
Spew them hence, oh wicked brow,
The source of all my madness and gladness!
I had no gods, only evil; let's away.
Ready to pounce under the power of eruption,
They disgraced a young child to the four winds.'

'Some disgrace,' I butted in:
'I took a breath I shall not prolong
To mount upon you and let out your cage.
You've sung a rave song in the year of birth,
And my sword shall pounce 'pon ye!'

I began to embrace her. I wanted to visit her below the shoreline, to enter
that piercèd hollow, but I knew damnably that I had to wait...

... and said this to her instead:
'Hie, my love, 'til we meet again
I cry for thee, not for whom you think
Death's still watch goes fleeing by the by
Likes beholden, lies me still
Lies that had comforted a cheap thrill.'

'I have no bosom with the air,' she stated, 'My wretched love is fit for thee.
The air is fair 'pon a pair, both in turn for thee.'

We kissed more rigorously. I sensed her longing for me, and with all she
said, sort of, I understood where she was coming from...

... she was just an ill-treated, reasonably-mannered, lonely girl who just wanted to be loved, just as Malone said...

... and that I shall give her, for I won't hear the end of it!

She asked me, 'Your parents nigh?'

'In th'eavens,' I told her. 'They died from a plague.'

'Too bad. It would have been nice to have a different set.'

'I think you would have liked them. Mother would have taken to you well. She did my first wife.'

'You were married before?'

'Well, yes, I was,' I reflected fondly with sadness, 'But she died too.'

'Same plague?'

'During the outbreak long ago.'

'I ran away long afore, cannot remember now when, anymore. It was a most lonesome ride.'

'Where did you go?'

'Northward. Anyward, only to get away from *them*.'

'Self-seeking devotion, I like that,' I sniggered.

'Well it was more self-preservation more than anything else.'

'Were they that bad?'

Her head lowered, with eyes raised toward me. *'Yes, they were. It would be constituted as abuse nowadays.'*

'I was told about that long ago. I shall nay allow such things to ever again happen to ye. In the time we've spent together, and our sentiments revealed, I believe we can conjoin to rule Cobhayr together.'

'Maybe creating a newer world among us?'

'Hey yeah, that would be most fine,' I agreed. 'But how are you on religious matters? There's that new wind still blowing.'

'And I want to catch that wind,' she insisted.

I was impressed. 'And so do I! I'll have to take you to a friend of mine, who can help in such matters.'

With that, I got up and looked out the window from my tall tower, looking for Devenel. The Square was bustling with endless activity, as all Squares of a town do. The people all looked a-mush with similarity, and it was difficult to differentiate between them all...

... but one person stood out among them.

A haggardly man with a long white beard, with his usual tatty brown-gown-about-town look, stood in the centre showing magic spells to the kids. Even despite the new religion, our old Celtic beliefs remained intact and were shared into the next generation...

... but who knew how long it would last.

'I found my friend, Cindy,' I said, pointing in Dev's direction, 'Would you like to meet him?'

'Who's this friend?'

'He's a druid named Devenel, and he may have contacts with the new wind.'

'All druids have contact with the wind, that's why they smell so,' she held her nose.

'Go on,' I chided, 'It's not like that, but I do agree with you that a bath would not go amiss for him.'

She giggled, and we went down together, headed for the Square.

CHAPTER XVII

When we met Devenel on the side lane where the tower was. He had revealed that both Cindihan and I had been under a spell, because he was worried about how we would get on. The hesitation and awkwardness about the whole situation sent klaxons ringing in the old man's mind. So, the old man, with the help of Ralstyn's folk, had the old magic playing out between us, during our time together in the tower. The spell explained the eloquence and poetic license our conversation took.

'I did not trust you alone with her, especially with the sentiments you expressed to me earlier. I knew there was something between you, but it was imperative for all that you fall in love. That's the way the sword had been drawn,' he explained.

The druid certainly had a way with words.

Yet, he still wanted to know more, as if we went out together. 'Did you enjoy your time with her?'

'I did enjoy the path set before me,' I rang with vigour, mimicking his flowery tongue.

'Good lad, I knew you'd come around.'

'Dev, I'm no lad, remember?'

'I do, but does she?'

Devenel and I looked at Cindy, who blurted, 'What?'

The old man asked, 'Are you aware of a still-age potion?'

Cindy didn't get it, obviously. 'Still-age?'

'This man you see before you; he looks similar in age to you presently, but he is a much, much older man,' Devenel said.

Now it was Cindy's time to worry. 'Are you telling me you have rigged me up with a fuellèd-fossil?'

'Nay, nay, princess,' I tried to explain. 'I am no fossil, but I am many years older than you, decades even. My age was stilled by a passing druid, like Devenel here, but she's left our scene.'

'Where'd she go?'

'To the beyond, where she communes better with the magic folk,' Devenel answered.

'Ah, she died,' Cindy concluded.

'You can say that, but you do not know the other worlds of the beyond,' Devenel added.

She got suspicious. 'Are you trying to pick me up?'

He got defensive. 'Good heavens, no child! You were picked by the fates to join with this gentleman to rule a better world for all of us.'

'Why would you want to do that? I'm not of royal lineage, nor of any noble-based either. I come from a...'

I sharply interrupted, 'Cindy, Cindy,' I put a finger to her lips. 'Stop. It took me a long while to get used to the idea that I was eternally matched with you.

'I have accepted the foretelling, spent time with fairy-folk to allow myself to know and understand the pain in your life. I can help you heal and rise above all stations.'

'Helps if there's something arriving at the station to begin with, unless they hadn't built it yet,' Cindy intoned.

I looked at Devenel. Her scepticism seeped through like a mesh bag full of wet laundry.

Devenel went up to the maid. 'Cindy dear, your station has been built, and not only that, you have an arrival due any minute.'

She then got excited. 'Really? Who?'

The old druid chimed, 'Right here. He's coming for you, he's coming for you.'

He then took me by the arm and thrust me in front of her.

'Here he is; your Conna.'

Her eyes had gave a *wow* response. 'All mine? No hitches?'

Devenel continued, 'As foretold in a future tense, which is now the present. Your years finally completed, you two are meet to unite, continuing Longsearch's line of power.'

Cindy repeated, 'Longsearch?'

'My father,' I said.

'Ah,' she acknowledged.

I put my arm around the lady. 'I think he would have liked you, even if you are the way you are.'

She asked, 'And how am I to you?'

'Ummm,' I smiled, looking back at Devenel, 'Meet to unite, continuing the line of power.'

Devenel laughed, 'And we shall drop the *O'Myde* nonsense. That name wasn't meant for you anyway, as the townsfolk bore naught against ye. You are Lowry Cindihan for all time.'

She got unsteady. 'Just like that?'

Devenel snapped his fingers, 'With magic, just like that! Now shut-it, and enjoy the love with Conna.'

We walked into the main road, toward the Square, when a throng of townsfolk enveloped us.

One shouted out, 'Word has it you're getting married. When's the wedding?'

Another yelled out, 'Are you our new King?'

More people cried, 'How will you rule over us?'

The queries blasted past us, as we walked away from them. I did not think there was much interest in my doings, but with Cindy in tow, I figured they would get the drift...

... I just wish they would drift away for now.

'I'm not getting any younger, there is none else for me,' Cindy lamented.

'No, neither am I, my love.' I held her hand to comfort her. 'My process will still my age for as long as...'

Devenel rudely interrupted our fine moment. 'For as long as absolutely necessary. You don't want your man to look like me, do you?'

She made a face and gazed at him. 'Ummm, no. I don't... old and shaggy-busted.'

'Old and shaggy-busted, indeed,' Devenel tutted back, with misplaced self-pride. 'Conna is a tad younger than me, but not by much. I could reverse the spell, you know.'

'Uh, no, no thanks,' she quickly reconsidered. 'I like Conna as he is. He is very beautiful, and wise-looking.'

'Dreamily handsome in a mid-centuried style,' Devenel assured.

My silence spoke volumes, as I tried to respond, but I giggled to myself over the attention I was being given. Spells could cheat age, it was a wonder if they could cheat Death itself. I wondered how long this 'age spell' would last, and whether my so-called youth would remain intact. I remembered Dev's earlier argument about it, and the *as long as absolutely necessary* attitude had to be accepted. Maybe he meant how far it can be stretched, as some magic can be most flexible, when need be...

... and with this situation brewing, I had a feeling that his was a very need-be cause.

Cindy gave me a hug and said, 'I love you, no matter what age y'are.'

'That's very kind of you my dear,' I gave her a kiss. 'I love you too.'

And this time, I was not under a spell.

Devenel watched us keenly, listening to the banter between us. 'I see you feel devotion to the lady, Conna. We must take the next step. I recall a conversation with you regarding the new wind that's blowing about our district, and the wider counties. While I had you posted to Seecleare, a new church had been founded, called *St Aidash*. I've spoken to the priest there, called Clivewood, and he is willing to initiate you both into the Church, and later, to trim your sheds.'

I blossomed out, 'Trim our sheds?'

'It is his odd way of expressing matrimony,' Devenel answered.

Cindy asked, 'Who's St Aidash?'

'A local lad was wickered recently for witchery. The matter was concluded by making him saint, as he was innocent of the charge. Unfortunately, the townsfolk were very suspicious of him and his ways.'

She made another face...

... as Devenel explained, 'It was during your spell away from Cobhayr, yours too, Conna. It was said that he spoke to cats, and he got wickered for it.'

'I think that's dumb,' Cindy protested. 'I like cats, and animals, and they deserve love and respect like people, because they are living beings.'

'Yes, and as a living being, I agree with you, but the majority does not,' he said. 'Most here believe animals are for purpose, not frippery.'

I frowned. 'So, what was the big deal?'

Devenel looked dour. 'The cats spoke back to him.'

A silence passed us, as I looked at Cindy and reflected in full horror what untamed human nature was capable of. It also gave me further insight toward what Cindy had gone through, in her previous time with the O'Mydes.

'Anyway,' Devenel broke the silence, 'Let's be off to see Clivewood.'

So we went off into another section away from town, down a street, up a hill, where the new congregation of *St Aidash* was formed.

CHAPTER XVIII

Father Clivewood was expecting us. He waited at the wooden doorway, as we approached *St Aidash* up it's winding path. He stood tall, as a reasonably gingerbread-sized fellow would. He waved to us, and warm greetings were exchanged.

'Welcome, Devenel,' Clivewood chimed, 'These are your two charges for me to initiate?'

'Yes,' Devenel answered him. 'We thoroughly discussed the matter, and it was thought the best way to move forward, for Cobhayr's sake.'

'Indeed, it is,' the priest agreed. 'Our congregants are growing pretty fast, and more churches are being built to accommodate our following. I trust you will be joining us as well?'

The old druid felt uneasy at this, not wishing to dispense the 'wild' ways of yore. 'I am too old in my beliefs to change now. My dear friends here, Conna and Cindihan, are your better targets. They shall be more willing for the change.'

'Good.' Clivewood led us into the church, where we sat in one of the wooden pews.

There were other followers scattered in the sanctuary, kneeling in prayer, wrapped up in devotion, personal concerns, or nervous paranoia, so they gave no notice to us.

Clivewood set his attention to Cindy and I. 'Your druid friend here says you are willing to be initiated into our Faith.'

I looked at him, hungry-eyed, now that I've finally found a path to tread upon. 'I do. I expect we will have many ceremonial dealings with you.'

The priest raised his eyebrows, yet expecting my request. 'Oh? Now how is that?'

'I am Conna of Cobhayr, son of Longsearch, the next King to be. I am to be called Muffyhuer, as my formal title, and Cindihan is to be my Queen. We'll have to get married and royally installed.'

'You'll get royally installed, all right,' Devenel addressed Cindy and I, 'First things first. Conna, Cindihan, are you ready to depart from our more uncivilised patterns?'

I stood confident, still sitting, 'I'll knock them out!'

'Atta boy, Conna.' Devenel patted me on the back. 'Now, Cindihan, what is your standing on this matter?'

Cindy was less assured about it all, though her intention was as true as my own; her past made things more volatile to her decision making...

... and I soon intervened on her behalf. 'She's a bit complex, you see, she'd been...'

Devenel cut in quickly. 'Ah, she'd been down a dimmer path, shall we say. No one practices the magic she had learned in her youth. That magic's now passed away, and so has her family. Conna is the only one she's got, and he is her new path.'

Clivewood asked Cindy, 'You are willing to join us?'

She cooed at the prospect of self-betterment. 'Oh yes, please!'

'Fine. It's agreed, then. Give me a bit of time to prepare for your baptisms, and then, maybe at the same time, we can trim your sheds for you.'

'I love it. It is like having a two in one ceremony,' I yelped.

'And we don't have much time,' Devenel added, 'We have to get you installed as King. So these little things must be done sooner, to get you both united.'

I felt love in my heart, which was growing for dear little Cindy. I came to her in good faith, and I would be happy to stay with her for many lifetimes together.

* * * * * *

I'd spent my time with Cindy, back in my old hovel of *Oh Konn Nahh*. Despite it being my former home with Lyola, I thought nothing of enjoying this once-loved space again, now that time had passed and I wasn't set asunder with bad memories of Lyola and Longjohn's deaths...

... especially that they weren't really dead in the first place.

I dismissed the pain of my past, and concentrated on getting Cindy over her own. I made space in my heart to continue wooing her, and this secret cave away from the rest of society, was a perfect remembrance of the wild times that lay beneath us. Our being together was most enriching, and Cindy did not display any of Lyola's elusive qualities. She was a completely different woman, with different feelings and meanings within her.

We didn't get too frisky with one another either; I wanted to save *that* for when it was temporally appropriate. There was the occasional fumble-around, but nothing of significance. I knew in my higher standing as King Muffyhuer-to-be, I'd have to be careful, for public opinion's sake.

A messenger came to us the following week, when we were called back to *St Aidash* for our baptismal/marriage ceremony. It was with the most willingness I'd ever expressed for myself. As the first Christian King of Cobhayr, it was a momentous feat. With Cindy as my Queen, it would be a real-time, enriching experience that would not be forgotten in a hurry.

A horse was provided for me and Cindy, and we rode out toward the small hill, just outside Cobhayr's edge, where the church was. It had its crowd of followers, who turned up to witness our dual event. I was unsure if any of the old Celtic, magical ways would wheedle their way into our union, but it would be fun if they did.

As we drew near, many voices arose, crying, 'Conna of Cobhayr, son of Longsearch; our King, our King!'

A 'royal' welcome was definitely enjoyed by me, as it was good of the people to acknowledge who I was. They also accepted Cindy, despite her ordeal with the O'Mydes, and were happy to see me with a woman who can be strong enough to serve the community, and forget about herself.

I dismounted, and helped Cindy down from the horse, and entered the church. The place was loaded with people from head to foot, as many of them were eager, not only to see us join them in Faith, but to see us wed, as well.

It was obvious I was getting on, and the onlookers marvelled at my handsomeness; even whispers about it floated around the sanctuary.

The magic spell Kitta had placed on me, did its job in keeping me forty years younger. If not for the spell, I would rival Devenel in years, because he was just a short hop older than me; I didn't want to look like him *now*.

Father Clivewood led everyone in prayers, thoughts, announcements, and community spirit. Devenel sat with Cindy and I in front, for moral support and guidance, as he'd always done. Though he would not partake in the ceremony, being duly just for Cindy and me, he wanted to see us happy in the path that was good for Cobhayr.

The service was moving, emphasising Christian ways, with a firm break from the past, as Clivewood stated:

'To accept Christ into the midst of our hearts, we let go of our wild selves, and transform ourselves within the new direction of Light.'

More prayers were prayed, said, chanted, sung, and soon, Cindy and I officially joined the ranks of Christendom in this year of our Lord 718. We were taken to the rear of the building, where there was a pool. The people gathered in the doorways, though some of them remained in the sanctuary, knowing they could 'hear' the initiation process.

Clivewood then continued, 'As new members-to-be, we reach out to Him who bore rough Mercy, giving way to our mortal turmoil. As a token of that esteem and judgement, I take these two wild oats, and sow them into the sea of life, creating something anew that rings with Your Love, Your Loyalty, and Your Destiny.'

Suddenly, we were stripped of our tunics to near naked, and pushed into the water with a huge splash, thus entering the Church on a very wet footing.

The greying, thick hair on my chest stood on end at the surprised moment, and Cindy giggled at me. We certainly took the plunge, and were about to make another plunge of another footing.

Clivewood asked Devenel, 'Have you the rings?'

Devenel fished in his tatty, but not torn pockets, for the rings that will seal us together in love and serious commitment to ourselves. The bargain I made with the druid will now be fulfilled; I took the steps for the sake of Cobhayr's future as its leader.

Clivewood took the rings from him, and said, 'Conna of Cobhayr, do you take Lowry Cindihan unto yourself, newly baptised, to cherish, have, hold and to rule Cobhayr, alongside you as your future Queen?'

It was the perfect double-barrelled vow I'd ever taken, 'I do.'

'Lowry Cindihan, do you take Conna of Cobhayr unto yourself, newly baptised, to cherish, have, hold and to rule Cobhayr, alongside you as your future King?'

'I do,' she affirmed.

'I now pronounce you man and wife, and both Christian. You may kiss your bride, Conna.'

Sodden and risen out of the water, we kissed endlessly. Devenel, Clivewood, and the few who got to see the full experience, clapped for us, giggling to themselves at our open intimacy. As we exited the pool, clinging to some fabric of modesty, Devenel had another laugh at us, and pushed us back in. Everyone burst out laughing.

When we bobbed back above, Devenel hovered over us. 'You must now be installed as our King and Queen. There's no turning back now.'

With all the commotion about us, we went out of the water, and went out the side door to dress and dry off in the summer sunshine. The indoor crowd now exited the church and went up to us to wish us well with infinite congratulations. Flowers were thrown at us, some even went up to us for a hug or kiss...

... but the chanting was even more profound.

'Our King, Muffyhuer, Muffyhuer!'

I looked back at Devenel, and realised he was correct...

... *there was no going back.*

CHAPTER XIX

Not too long after our wedding, our regal lives began. The councilmen of the township, along with Devenel, had long prepared me over the years for leadership, and now that Cindy's on board, the ship was about to sail forth. In my younger years (after Dad had passed away), I served on the council for a long time, as the Successor of Cobhayr. The members had waited for me to find the one who was to be my Queen, before installing me as King of Cobhayr.

I was in my tower, having a cool contemplation. Cindy cleaned up a few things, dusting off the corners, when Devenel entered the humble room. Despite all the responsibilities about to be put upon me, I wanted to spend more time with Cindy, alone, and stated so.

'Nay, lad,' Devenel commanded, 'Your status must serve first.'

I moaned and groaned under my breath, when the old fellow handed me a bulky parcel.

I looked at it keenly. 'What is this?'

'You may recognise it when it's opened.'

I cut the string with a small hunting knife, that I still had from when I was going on hunts with Dad. With the paper wrapping lain aside, a glimmer of golden brown fur glinted at me with familiarity.

I cried, 'Dad's old formal suit!'

'It is to become your investiture outfit. During your time in Seecleare, Kitta and I had worked in making it fit for you. We'd made some modifications and mending to preserve it for your forthcoming day. It was the last thing she did before she died. Try it on.'

'No way, Dev,' I protested, still reeling from the memory, 'This is Dad's.'

'Not anymore, son,' Devenel reassured me. 'It has been made for you specifically, and it shows you as the successor of Longsearch. Now, please stop fussing about it and try the damn thing on!'

I sighed, backing down, and went into another small room to do the deed. When I came out, I was unable to speak. The suit still had too much of Dad in it.

'You look splendid,' Devenel beamed, 'Ah, your father would have been proud of you. Turn around.'

I spun on my heel slowly, letting the old man check out the newly cleaned golden brown fur; the silver trim; the shine of the insignias; the intricately braided cloak; the furry, silver trimmed hat; along with the silver boots and gloves.

I asked hurriedly, wishing to take it off. 'So the suit fares well on me, eh?'

'You look like a prime target for a good chase. Cindihan!?'

The lady looked up from her tasks, 'Yes?'

Devenel addressed her. 'What do you think of this succulent splendour?'

Her eyes widened, as she touched the furry sides, the metallic middle, the bumpy braid of the cloak and the smoothness of the shiny silver trim.

'It fits, it fares, and Conna looks extraordinarily attractive,' she gushed at the dazzle of the spectacular suit.

'A fine secretion of a divine being,' Devenel equally gushed.

Now I couldn't figure out what was going on between them, nor understood what Devenel meant by *secretion*, but I took it as a compliment.

Cindy then slapped me on the rear and ran down the stairs, heading outside.

'Well, the chase is on,' Devenel invited, 'Good luck to ye.'

I excused myself to run after her, running and searching for this crazy woman, who was now my wife.

The chase led us toward the Square, where many people bustled in their daily chores of life. We clumsily bumped into a few, apologies pronounced, as our little game had played out in public.

One onlooker observed, 'Wasn't that Conna and Cindihan?'

Another shared his interlude. 'The marriage must suit them well. They cannot get away from one another. I tried doing that to my missus and we hadn't got far. She caught me a few feet away!'

'I hadn't gotten out of my house before my missus caught me,' revealed another.

We chased each other away from the nostalgia of marital chasing, past the benches, when we took a breather.

'Your turn,' she called.

'Cindy, we're not children. This is hardly fitting for us to do.'

'I thought women were supposed to chase men about.'

'That's in the courting stage. We're past that now.'

She blew a raspberry at me, and continued the playful moment. *Well, if two could play at this.*

I snuck up behind her, kissed her, then slapped her on the rear, like she did me.

'Darn you Conna, come back to me. I'll get you yet,' she shouted out.

I ran and ran in my regal best (or should I say *Dad's*). To be honest, I sure felt silly, running around in this hot suit and wondered what Dad would have said if he saw me running around like a crazy bun, chasing a small lady, in his formal of formals.

'Let her work for her keep,' he'd say, *'And chase ye into eternity.'*

Dad had a strange way of looking at things.

We made it back to the tower in one piece, even the suit. We were panting like mad dogs after a betting race.

'You've made it,' Devenel greeted. 'I can see Kitta and I done a good job on the suit. You can run in it. Very good.'

'This was not an expected pleasure,' I assured him. 'Cindy started it.'

She stuck her tongue out in jest, and cried, 'Spoil sport!'

'Nyahh,' I answered her with one.

'Now now, you two, you've had your fun. I told you she'd give you chase. You are a rather attractive fellow; Kitta's still-age spell remains intact upon you.'

I turned to my baser instincts, turned to Cindy and drew upon her face a very fine, intimate kiss. She put her hands on my furry shoulders, leaning in to receive me.

Devenel thought it too much at once. 'Alright kids, that's enough.'

We were both still panting from the chase, then moaned at Devenel's complaining.

'It's about time you saw sense,' he then scolded, 'You are about to become the new King. What was your example of running around the town for?'

'To give good chase, as you stated,' I answered, knowing it was *his* idea. 'Besides, we wanted a bit of fun. I do not want to be a stuffy old King. I am a new shining star of a person.'

'That's due to the potion, you know, and I can still have it reversed. You will then become a stuffy rag, old hag bag like me,' he warned.

I stood still and silent. Then sat next to Cindy.

'It's about time we made you King and Queen. Your ceremony is upon you,' Devenel said.

* * * * * *

It was a cool autumn day, when our final ceremony had begun. I was dressed up in Dad's refurbished formal. Everyone marvelled at the sparkle of it, but I just saw it as a mangy old suit. Cindy wore a long sleeve green top, which came up to her neck, under a long blue tunic with pretty Celtic patterns bordering the edges. A gold cross-shaped brooch was placed on her left side, by her heart. Her hair flowed bountifully along her shoulders. her shoes were black, and covered her feet to keep her warm. My coverings kept me warm too, but I thought of another way to keep warm with her. I daren't think of that now at our installation.

A surviving member from the families of the Backnah Valley officiated the ceremony. This one, descending from Lloyd, was named Leiwulf. He lived his life mostly at the castle taken from King Fynne long ago, and left unaffected during that plague outbreak. I didn't think any of them survived, but with large families, it is likely *someone* will emerge in the future.

He had Cindy and I called up to receive our new station in life:

'It is with great pleasure that I install Conna of Cobhayr, son of Longsearch, as King Muffyhuer, along with Lowry Cindihan as his Queen. Muffyhuer is a term specific to you Conna, as your regal address. May the hairy happiness of your heart lead Cobhayr along a finer path to a new world.'

Leiwulf then handed over the relics of officialdom; the sceptre and the orb. Cindy got a sceptre too, *but the orb was all mine.*

'You are now installed as King and Queen of Cobhayr, Muffyhuer and Cindihan,' he announced proudly.

Father Clivewood, in his position as religious leader, anointed us with a holy oil, a heartfelt prayer, and goodwill to our future together. He wished us a long, blessèd, and inspiring reign. The crowd in the Square emitted whoops and cheers, with applause surrounding the sounds of all. Devenel gave us both a hug and advised us to get on with our honeymoon, before the lively tone of the moment evaporates...

... so we made our escape, with provided horse, and returned to our makeshift cave of *Oh Konn Nahh*.

CHAPTER XX

Thankfully, Devenel was gracious enough to give us some time to ourselves. We lived at *Oh Konn Nahh* and spread across its environment, taking in the splendour and the majestic valley of Backnah below. I walked with Cindy to take in the green, patchwork landscape, and marvelled at the nature around us. In doing so, we kept in touch with the wild side of *our* nature.

I sat down next to her on a rock beside a stream. We did a bit of fishing, caught one, and had breakfast. On another occasion, we laid out on the grass besides the cave of *Oh Konn Nahh*. There, we had a fumble and a turn, then we kissed.

I asked her, 'So how do you like being my Queen?'

'I love it. The sun always shines on this side of the throne,' she answered.

I laughed at the remark, but wondered if she truly meant it.

'Then, with all the dishevelment of your past life Cindy, was it worth it?'

She paused to reflect. 'As long as it's a one-way system, so there's no turning back and infecting others with it.'

'With what?'

'My past, duh!'

I grinned. 'Ye cannot turn back. They are dead, and their whole family's been dispersed back into the wider continent, east of us; if not, already dead. There shall be no further bother from them, my lass.'

'Well, I do thank you for your help, despite your earlier reservations about me.'

'I didn't mean to be so difficult. My first wife turned out to be a fairy; she was very elusive about this. It was when she died, I had realised what she was. I felt I was cheated badly, so when I saw you as a young child on the boat, and my cohorts had told me that you were the one, the hardship it took on my part to accept this was insurmountable.'

She had an idea. 'You can mount this, then.'

Her suggestion brought me closer to her, and I removed the belt from my tunic to loosen up. I was secretly proud of her dismissive attitude.

I came even closer to the skin, or clothing at least, as she got more comfortable with me. After a few more rounds of fussing about, I released myself to enter discreetly into her holy portal. I looked around in a rave to make certain no one was around...

... and there were no people; firstly it was early morning, second, no one really gave a toss, for everyone did it at all hours.

The burden of status was put aside for while, as for all Kings and Queens, an heir must be created...

... and so it was, as I gently scaled upward and moved about inside her.

She held onto me tightly, without squeezing.

We took it in turns, pleasuring one another. I kept feeling a minor sensation, coming from somewhere, *but it was not where it was supposed to be.*

I felt my face, which by now showed signs of sagging, compared to the youthful tightness from before. My body began to do likewise, despite all the years of holding together well. Yet, I was changing quicker than the wily teenager I once was...

... and I think I've become a ninety year old man in seconds!

The potion was fading! Devenel told me it would, someday, in his crazy manner, even threatening to end it. The forty years hold I was promised had dwindled, fast. Cindy didn't notice it, as she looked as if in a trance. Maybe it was love, maybe it was another spell...

... maybe she just didn't look.

Her agèd youth shared inside stood still and sure of itself. Like a castle guardsman, it did not yield. I guess she liked it that way. I, on the other hand, was becoming more antiquated by the moment. It was a most cruel notion, *to age while mating*. My breath felt short, my body began to feel weakened, and soon, I had a sinking feeling...

...it was me going underground.

It was a living death. I felt vile about it and ashamed, once I realised what was happening to me. *I was becoming the earth!* I glanced at Cindy to see if anything was a-flutter with her...

... nope, same ol' Cindy, an older woman hastening to get old, and still on top of the ground.

Suddenly, she felt something too, as the ground was moving beneath her, sinking.

'Conna, what's happening to us?' She took a good look at the changed man I'd become, and screamed, 'CONNA!'

'It's alright, dear,' I gasped, as I held her. 'It's the potion. It's wearing off. Remember, I told you that when I was waiting for you to come to fruition, Dev's friend and fellow magic hag, Kitta gave me a potion to stay my age. I had been middle-aged for years. Now those years have caught up with me, and this is how I really am today. I've come to term.'

Cindy then noticed our bodies were slowly sinking into the ground.

'And so we are,' she observed, 'Look.'

Our bodies became entangled like vines in an unkempt ivy bush, savagely growing on a building. We held unto one another, in an attempt to survive.

'No, this cannot be,' I cried out.

A booming voice had called overhead. *'Conna, your time has come to join the gods. I do not care which one you believed in, or who you believe in now. You have abandoned us for the new wind a-blowing. Conna, son of Longsearch, you are hereby claimed by the true gods of your ancestors. And tough shit about your wee little girlfriend. If she loves you that much, she'll be willing to die with you.'*

'Conna, I'm scared,' Cindy shouted.

The violence set forth upon us was no match for what was to come.

'Hold me, child, dear child. You yourself don't deserve this. My father pissed off the gods years ago, and they cursed him with flame.

'Now, the claim is upon me, and whom I love. They're coming for us. I am so sorry it had to end this way.'

'As long as we're together forever, we'll bunk up in eternity,' she compromised.

'I'd like that, but we will no longer rule Cobhayr. All shall change with our passing.'

Soon, the earth swallowed up more of our bodies, as we kept tighter against each other.

'Conna, I love you so much.' She then kissed me.

Nearing our cruel end, I vowed with all my heart, 'I'll love you forever, Cindihan; our names shall be remembered in the future.'

Another seismic movement occurred when the earth slumped over us, and Cindy screamed one final time, *'OH CONNA!'*

Then, we were both at one with the earth. There was no trace, no body, no being. All that was left was a salty-dog day, sniffing the ends of the earth, and a pathway leading up to a greater salvation.

* * * * *

The call of 'Oh Conna!' was heard in the forthcoming wind, and lodged deeply in its throat. The call spread for miles around within Cobhayr district, all the way to the Backnah Valley. A man named Leiwulf, whose family originated from the Backnah Valley long before, still kicked around, though his family had long since departed. He was the one who installed Conna and Cindihan as King and Queen of Cobhayr.

Just after the King and Queen's pitiful demise, he was walking around with his pet dog, Mooshie, when the wind revealed the echoed calling. The cry was intense, and as grim as death.

Mooshie barked loudly at the sound, which attracted Leiwulf.

'What's the matter, Moosh? You smell or hear something?'

The animal showed intense discomfort, and looked in the direction where the sound came from.

Leiwulf went back home and got on his horse, racing toward the area as if he were in a betted race, only to find...

... nothing. Absolutely nothing.

A big patch of new brown soil was left within the surrounding greenery of the land. Mooshie ran to the patch and sniffed it fiercely, barking like a madman (if he had been one).

Leiwulf dismounted and hitched the horse on a tree stump and looked around him. The cave of Oh Konn Nahh was now deserted, but he took a look there anyway, just in case. He knew who lived there (Conna aka King Muffyhuer and Queen Lowry Cindihan), and saw what was left from them and stayed silent. He didn't touch anything, nor seal the cave itself. He felt someone else would use it someday as an already furnished dwelling...

... and housing did not come easy back then, and still doesn't today.

Leiwulf rode away, with Mooshie chasing after him. The wind still choked with the death cry of Cindihan, 'Oh Conna!'.

He didn't understand why, but was fully aware of the antics of the old Celtic deities, that embodied so many human aspects and traits of the natural world. It was scary to deal with them on a normal basis, it was worse when you piss one or all of them off. They'd vow to take you alive as final payback for dishonour, or even on a whim.

Leiwulf thought about his recent experience of making Conna and Cindihan, King and Queen of Cobhayr. He liked the couple, and was very fond of Devenel, who recently let go his years. Leiwulf felt a tribute to the King and Queen was necessary, so they will be remembered for all time. With the ravaged cry still whistling in the wind, he thought about them and toyed about with their names until he came up with Oconnalow, the 'low' bit coming from Cindihan's first name, Lowry. He fashioned to petition the municipality to rename Cobhayr to Oconnalow, out of respect for the former King and Queen.

The new name was pitched to the townsfolk, and makeshift leadership, after the King and Queen had passed on. The people and leaders liked the name, as it had a good ring to it and fully acknowledged both in tribute. There was a hopeful future in the new identity of the township.

The Cobhayr of old had now faded away, along with all that it represented of the antiquated orders. The new wind of Christendom had not only gripped the township, but of all of Ireland itself. The sweetness of it embraced in the bosom of many, who accepted its message of confidence and hope. The old gods had passed from their minds, and took with them those who they saw fit to devour, as a last stand...

... Muffyhuer and Cindihan.

With the deaths of King Muffyhuer and Queen Cindihan, Leiwulf was promoted to become the new leader of Oconnalow.

It was a proud occasion for him. Leiwulf's family lived here forever, being the only survivor of the old order. Yet, he knew to go forward and disperse with the dark age myths that remained in darkness, because recent folk didn't care about them anymore.

During all the changes occurring in the land, something else emerged that was new. It was not just the new name of Oconnalow, nor the new faith in Christ, but a baby. This baby came from that dark patch of earth where Conna and Cindihan once stood, and got consumed by. The baby was a boy, and he wailed something awful. He couldn't protect himself, nor was there anyone around to see to his needs...

... until a young maiden girl, late in her teens, passed by on her daily walk, and heard the dominant cry.

When she saw the child, she squealed, 'Oooh, a child! Who the heck would abandon you, such a beautiful infant bunny. You're so cute, and I'm going to wrap you up and take you back to my place.'

She had a gold coloured, fleece-lined shawl on her, which she used to cover up the baby with. He was nice and snugly, and at least one of his wishes was fulfilled.

She asked the baby rhetorically, 'So where are your folks?'

The babe didn't answer. It couldn't, and she knew that. She was just horsing around, and having fun with the new-found bundle.

The wind then embraced its dark refrain. 'OH CONNA!'

'Conna,' she whispered, repeating the name, 'Conna. Hey, would you like to be called Conna? Conna Daye, because Daye is my name. I bet you'd love that, wouldn't you. Nature itself gave you that name.'

The baby cooed and fussed, then grizzled because it got hungry.

'We'll be getting home soon. I see there is no one here, and that some dopey horror had abandoned you.'

If only she knew of the real circumstances the gods befell upon the parents of little Conna!

She walked away with Conna, hugging him and keeping him in that gold coloured, fleece-lined shawl. It was chilly, but she didn't care. She was tough and strong in her body. The child was not. The young girl Daye returned home with little Conna, where her family accepted and raised this sprout of the gods.

Since finding Conna, Miss Daye remained not harried, and undisturbed in the quiet peace and calm of the day. The gods, too, remained silent, though observant. Just because no one believed in them, did not mean they no longer existed. They could exist, if one believed...

... but by now, no one did...

... however, there was just one more occasion, where the screech of the gods was heard.

When the little baby Conna Daye grew up many years later, and affirmed in his manhood, the gods had one final word for him, during Conna's bipedal discourse with the earth:

'Conna Daye, you are the first of the new lineage, the fruit of the earthen remains of King Muffyhuer, formerly Conna of Cobhayr, and Queen Lowry Cindihan. We took them to ourselves, leaving you as their legacy, along with their names. For all time, you and any direct descendant, be it man or woman, must perform the Sacred Rite of Oconnalow. This is to remember the love they had for each other and to ensure that love between your parents follows to you, and any you love or will love, for all time.'

The voice quieted down, the last of its breath being extinguished. The old order was forever silenced in mystery...

... and now Conna Daye had some begetting to do.

CPSIA information can be obtained
at www.ICGtesting.com
Printed in the USA
BVHW071508110920
588613BV00001B/249